A BIRD IN THE AIR MEANS WE CAN STILL BREATHE

Also by Mahogany L. Browne

Chlorine Sky

Vinyl Moon

A BIRD IN THE AIR MEANS WE CAN STILL BREATHE

MAHOGANY L. BROWNE

Crown ♛ New York

Text copyright © 2025 by Mahogany L. Browne
Jacket art copyright © 2025 by Cymone Wilder
Map art copyright © 2025 by David Cooper
Jacket photo copyright © 2025 by Ryan DeBerardinis/Shutterstock
Jacket design by Ray Shappell

All rights reserved. Published in the United States by Crown Books for Young Readers, an imprint of Random House Children's Books, a division of Penguin Random House LLC, New York.

Crown and the colophon are registered trademarks of Penguin Random House LLC.

Visit us on the Web! GetUnderlined.com

Educators and librarians, for a variety of teaching tools, visit us at
RHTeachersLibrarians.com

Library of Congress Cataloging-in-Publication Data is available upon request.
ISBN 978-0-593-48647-4 (trade)—ISBN 978-0-593-48649-8 (ebook)

The text of this book is set in 11.5-point Adobe Garamond Pro.
Interior design by Cathy Bobak

Printed in the United States of America
10 9 8 7 6 5 4 3 2 1

The authorized representative in the EU for product safety and compliance is
Penguin Random House Ireland, Morrison Chambers, 32 Nassau Street,
Dublin D02 YH68, Ireland, https://eu-contact.penguin.ie.

Random House Children's Books supports the First Amendment
and celebrates the right to read.

Penguin Random House values and supports copyright. Copyright fuels creativity, encourages diverse voices, promotes free speech, and creates a vibrant culture. Thank you for buying an authorized edition of this book and for complying with copyright laws by not reproducing, scanning, or distributing any part of it in any form without permission. You are supporting writers and allowing Penguin Random House to continue to publish books for every reader. Please note that no part of this book may be used or reproduced in any manner for the purpose of training artificial intelligence technologies or systems.

To the young people,
may we always remember your bravery.
To the essential workers,
may we always bang pots in your honor.
To my mother, Ms. Ellaine,
this one is for you.

CONTENTS

NEW YORK

HARLEM

BRONX

RIKER'S ISLAND

HUDSON RIVER

EAST RIVER

QUEENS

MANHATTAN

FORT GREENE PARK

SAL'S

BED-STUY

BARCLAYS

BROOKLYN

Chorus: Wild Fire

If you listen closely, you can hear their TV screens pour from the windowpanes, under the apartment doors, and out onto the streets. Everybody is listening to the news, and no one is listening to their hearts.

I am Hyacinth.

Mi a har best fren, Electra.

And we're just two city girls . . .

Suh yuh sey, Ms. Trini-to-the-bone!

Okay, okay. We're two city girls with island roots. We met in the foster care system, after one too many fights took us from our families' homes and placed us as roomies in a group home slash detention center, wearing blue crew neck sweatshirts and matching sweatpants with one-size-too-small slippers. We sat in that weird-smelling facility until we were moved to neighboring foster care homes. Some might say we have a chip on our shoulders because we talk the truth loud. But really, we are over being talked down to, talked over, and completely ignored.

Fi Chuu.

You can say that being height-challenged brought Electra and me closer. Because for some reason, people think they can pick on people like us.

Dem pick pon mi, mi wi fight dem.

But you aren't here to hear about our origin story—you are here to learn the stories of how we all got to this weird pandemic phase in the first place. And you are in luck, because we keep our eyes wide open!

Serious. Wi see all a it.

No lies, we've seen it all. Okay, maybe not *all*—but a lot. Follow us. We have seen a granny spoon-feed VapoRub to a likkle one. We have seen fishermen pull seaweed from the mighty waters, clean all the sand free from the leaves, and make a cure with it. We have even seen a mother strap a baby on her back with thick kente fabric and machete a clearing through the sugarcane field for her family's safe passage to New York City.

She and Electra's mother moved from Kingston, Jamaica. And after my father passed away, my mother, big brother, big sister, and I moved from Trinidad and Tobago to Stamford, Connecticut.

We fine each odda unda strange circumstances.

Yes, Electra, we did find each other.

After we were both Scarlet Lettered as disruptive students (simply because we asked questions and demanded answers), we became used to being ignored. Adults often ignore the young people they don't understand. And this is when you really see the trees from the forest. This is why Electra and I are **chorus.** We have seen it all.

Like duppy. People figet sey wi deh yah.

We have seen   People living behind surgical masks
               waiting for the world to end
               People hoarding food and hand sanitizer
               People afraid to be kind to other people.

I mean, we weren't alive to witness the world surrender to the "Spanish" flu of 1918, the flu in 1957, or the flu in 1968. We only know what this rebuilt world looks like. And we know how to be good neighbors. We know to always be kind and say thank you. We know one should wait until everyone at the table has their meal in front of them before taking a bite. And we know we need each other to make the future possible.

Tank goodness we did raise fi know betta.

Malachi: Quinies, Part 1

It's like one day, the planet woke up and evicted us all.

One day we woke up and didn't have to go to school. It was just over. My entire freshman year in high school, poof! Gone. My brother, an extremely annoying eighth grader: Maseo Jr., formerly known as Lil Maseo but now known as MJ, didn't have school either. It was like we went to sleep angry about a test or whoever didn't text us back, or whoever was cowardly enough to write someone else's name on the bathroom wall in the locker room, and woke up to nothing.

Sure, the adults tried to pretend they knew what to do. Started online class check-ins a week later. But most of the students figured out quickly, if you turn your camera on to a pre-saved picture, then you might actually get some real work done on your current game of *Fortnite*. And sure, the adults tried to pretend they weren't stressed out, weekly deliveries of wine bottles and face masks tossed everywhere our shoes weren't. It lasted for a couple of months, until the Wi-Fi cut out. And we tried to stay on top of it all, but essential workers were quitting left and right. So finally, the phone towers were taken over by the ivy and various green waves of nature. It's like the earth opened her eyes one day and was tired of all our plastic straws and Amazon deforestation and cracked dirt from black oil and minerals mining.

First, we were told it was a new strain of flu. One that made your chest fill up with water and mucus. One cough and the fire would plant a little firecracker seed in the base of your neck. In two days, the seed sprouted and began to crawl up your spine into the back of your skull and stretch all its legs across your brain. The adults thought this new strain would only affect old people and poor people. Only some of them were upset. But the ones who stood outside of senior citizen homes with handmade signs and teary faces weren't upset; they were devastated. The news would plaster this picture on the screen and run every couple of hours. It was like a warning for us to stay home. The warning only seemed to work on people who cared about the elderly. Turns out, the president—my mama called him "that mean man"—was on the television screen with a red tie and orange face, instructing people to do homemade science experiments on themselves.

I asked Mama, "Why is he so mean? What's the difference between him and the rest of the people in charge?" She stopped cooking slices of turkey bacon on the stove and looked in the corner like the answer might live between the pop and the sizzle of our breakfast.

"He abuses his power. He told people to inject bleach to kill the virus! Like it was a joke." She scoffs. "What did I tell you about cleaning supplies?" She goes back to tending to the sizzle on top of the open fire.

"No drinking cleaning supplies," I chant like a song I don't like but know by heart because it plays on the radio every hour of every day.

"Malachi, I taught you that in kindergarten," she exclaims, shaking her head. "It's like some folks forgot the basics and just listen to anything these days. But they can't see anyone who makes hate speech is doing it for profit. And money doesn't care about the sick—as long as the bottom line isn't affected. You just watch. This kind of talk ain't no different than what your great-great-grandfather went through when they tried to take his land and his dog back in Louisiana. He prevailed, and we kept that land in the family despite them trying to ruin the soil and spoil the crops. People like that only listen to one thing: money. This is just the beginning!"

She balances her weight on her bad foot. You can tell it's bad because it's the only foot that swells like a bag of potato chips that's been in the bodega window too long. She shifts her weight and keeps talking. "In other places around the world, this sickness is happening, and no one is being forced to work. They are allowed to take care of their families and their health. But not this so-called leader. Oh no, he wants us back at work as if money is more important than people."

I nod like I understand, but I don't understand any of this, not really. As far as I could tell, Brooklyn has always been this way. Some rich people live there, and right across from them are ready-made millionaires in public housing. We all go to the same bodega. We all order from the same Chinese food spot. I just thought some of us got a doorman and some of us got a cigarette lady welcoming us home. But Mama is kind of telepathic because she answers the thoughts in my head.

"You may not notice the difference now. But as you grow older, you will see the difference, soon enough. Just keep your eyes open. See everything."

And just then the man with the worst advice ever says take a daily dose of a drug that people with lupus need. And I had to look it up for a research paper back when we were still in virtual school. A six-syllable word that made everybody catch their breath: hydroxychloroquine. It costs so much people started selling their food stamps for half the price, just to afford a month's supply. The manufacturers and bootleggers were selling it under the counter, online and rationing it out like it was water in a desert. Then the bootleggers began to see unprecedented profits and decided to split the drug with other substances to make it stretch, so they could make even more money.

This is when people started disappearing. We would be in our online classes and parents would have to do a "check-in" at the end of the week. Some of the parents' screens were just fuzzy static. Once where a concerned or tired face peered into the screen, now nothing. At first, me and my friends joked during *Fortnite* "zombies." And then one of the *Fortnite* players stopped laughing with us. It got eerily quiet.

The avatar stopped moving on the screen and everything, and a voice called out, "They're not zombies. And she might be a Quinie—but she's my mother no matter what."

Playing the game after that got really tense.

"Sorry. Maybe someone in the neighborhood has seen her?" I asked.

But deep down, I knew, people had already stopped talking to each other on the street weeks ago. Wearing masks around your face to keep the sick away was one thing, but when you were walking around afraid someone would rob you or hurt you (even if you weren't wearing a mask), they became even more distant and rude. No more holding doors open for one another. No more good-morning greetings when passing each other on the street. I was still thinking about how masks and sunglasses could make you feel more invisible than you might already feel, especially if you live in my part of Brooklyn. Especially if you look the way I do.

The voice cracked through the headphones. "I can't find her. I looked everywhere, even in the dark alleys near DUMBO. You know where the bridge arch is blocked? I can't find her anywhere. It's just not funny, that's all. I gotta go."

And that was that. We all stopped talking that day. I stopped playing altogether a few weeks later. Something about playing a game of strategy and death in silence makes it feel too real. Ever since then, I've been haunted by the voice that cracked on the other side of the headset. I mean, I consider myself lucky. I never had to think about what happened to Quinies. When I started to look more closely, or as Mama instructed, "see everything," the stories appeared everywhere.

Personal accounts of how these parents, aunts, uncles, cousins, sisters, brothers all just disappeared. And the people living with lupus ran out of ways to get their medication. Before, the drug was inexpensive and easily accessible. But now, the illegal drug is as hard to come by as a bar of gold. Everybody was living in the shadows of their misplaced dreams. But the people with lupus didn't disappear. They just became unalive.

My mother's best friend, Akeena Sil Lai, had lupus. But we are never allowed to call her anything but Auntie Akeena. She used to watch us kids when Mama had to work at the beer factory in Newark. Which was the worst because Mama had a two-hour train and bus commute, which means she was always tired. But yeah, we couldn't even go to Auntie Akeena's funeral. It was too dangerous to go outside. You never know what you're gonna walk into. So, Mama let us light a candle and put it in the window.

That night, it was so still. I didn't even hear the rats scouring the streets. No loud motorcycles tearing up and down the street playing DMX's *Greatest Hits*. It seemed no laughter or music that didn't already live in your own body existed. It's been like this for months now.

One day, maybe the third day after Auntie Akeena had passed away, Mama lit the candle and went to prepare breakfast before a big whoosh from the other side of the window blew the candle out. It was the first movement we felt in a long time. It was like a big mouth pushed out a big gust of air and made it all go dark.

Malachi: Quinies, Part 2

The adults had it wrong.
They thought it was a pandemic that we would all survive.
"Once it gets hotter, it'll be just fine!" they said.

People started having picnics as the virus mutated and evolved.
We thought we could evolve with it. Businesses opened outdoor
seating where black garbage cans once congregated, and repur-
posed sparkling water bottles holding a fistful of dying flowers
positioned in the center of their tables became a brunch scene.
People lined St. Marks Place in the city where the road was so
uneven, we would pretend the potholes were booby traps and
we attempted to hop each unnatural divot with one foot on the
pedal and one in the sky—prepared to make our spill the fun-
niest thing we talked about on the ride back across the red fated
bridge to Brooklyn.

The mayor said, "Get ready for summer!"
The racist president said, "Summer will kill the virus."

The governor said, "Be kind to each other and mask up."
The medical doctor who was older and frail-looking laughed at them all. He said, "It's a virus. It cannot be reasoned with."

The adults had it all wrong. They thought they could laugh, swipe right, and play away.
That we would all get it and some of us would be fine, and most of us would get sick, and hopefully, for those that could afford the medicine, the sick would heal.

The virus said, "50,000 dead. 135,000 sick."
The virus said, "110,000 dead. 1 million sick."
The virus said, "205,000 dead. 58 million sick."
The virus said, "500,000 dead in the United States. 102 million sick."
The medical doctor, who was old and frail, looked sad. He looked like someone who didn't want to play the "I told you so" game.

The virus had the last laugh. It kept on evolving without us. It would undo the majority of us first. Those of us who survived the undoing, those of us who canceled our weekly brunch traditions, those of us who refused to stay indoors began gathering outside for picnics and bench dates; those of us who survived played with dogs that weren't ours and let them nuzzle us like old friends—we found out what true longing looked like.

Longing for a sky that wasn't streaked with smog. The air quality condensed like milk and sour dreams. Longing for crushes to crush back the week after next. Longing for hugs. Longing for connection.

It is a scientific fact that humans need four hugs a day to survive. Word to world-renowned therapist Dr. Satir and my middle school homework for that gem. So, as the virus stretched out its limbs and put its bags down for a long stay, I took notice.

We started talking to our plants. When they didn't talk back, we sang to the plants, and sometimes they danced in the air; sometimes they died anyway. "They were always going to go," a voice in my head or on the TV said. We adopted pets. We crowned the pets with human names: Oliver, Patty, Kunta, Raheem. We made the fur babies our real babies. Let them hold all the emotions of angst and fear in their furry paws, or placed our frightened hands to the wetness of their snout until we felt safe. We laughed with them while watching reruns of *Living Single* and *Friends, Cheers* and *Dick Van Dyke*. There was nothing new on TV, because no one was working.

We were all waiting for the virus to get tired of feasting on our family members and loved ones. We were all waiting for the virus to die.

We have been waiting for the world to go back to "normal," but the virus is gluttonous. It ravaged over two-thirds of the globe, and still, no cure is in sight. I read in the online newspaper back when we still had Wi-Fi that there were cases of the virus found live in birds and bats.

In two weeks, we will have waited for two years for the virus to leave us alone. In two weeks, it will be a year since I last saw Mama. In two weeks, I turn eighteen. This is supposed to be the happiest moment of my teens. My senior year became a double junior/senior track because of all the school I missed.

Mama told me, "You are too brave to fail." Then tell me why this feels like the scariest time of my life.

Malachi: Quinies, Part 3

They thought it would only affect the poor people.

They thought it would only affect the ones that lived three blocks from my family and me. They didn't think the disaster would ever touch the other side of the biggest park in Brooklyn, not in a real way. But when the water began overflowing houses in the Upper West Side of Manhattan and the mountains of the commuter towns near Canada, something in the air snapped. That sound sent the rich to their vacation homes miles and miles away from the city, only to watch Lake Erie rupture its original path on its way back home to the Atlantic. Have you ever heard an earthquake marry a tornado? It sounded just like that, whooshing and quaking and cars screeching and screaming; it's like a wave hit and just passed down from person to person until we could all feel the rumble on the East Coast. A sound so deafening I was sure I would never hear a human's voice again.

First, the takeout shops ran out of food. Then the takeout shops boarded their doors, hoping a loan or a miracle would bring them back to the neighborhood. Then those same boards were used for firewood, after looters took anything worth saving. Cash registers were toys. ATMs were ransacked, then dragged through the streets behind pickup trucks for fun, while fires burned down houses on each side of the street. Houses that were set to flame once had a red X on the door. To let the world know: Someone here is affected by the virus. Be careful. Don't trespass. We have no cure.

Then the water came. Rushing all at once. Folks took to their boats, if they had them. And if they didn't, they climbed to the top of their roofs until the water took them to their final resting place.

The planes were grounded.
The water stayed for long.

We considered ourselves lucky. We had five floors to separate us from the water. The old couple in the basement apartment weren't so lucky. And anything below the third floor was considered a wash. Literally.

Have you ever smelled water that sat in itself, no place to go, for weeks?
For months?

Jeez, I miss the smell of salt in the air.

Mama once said, "The ocean is coming back for what is rightfully hers."

"Is that why Rockaway Beach was so dirty?" I asked.

She laughed. "It isn't clear blue like Jamaica, but it is ours. Be kind to the water. It's the people that tamper with its natural beauty."

MJ, who never really bothered with any discussion that didn't include Transformers as the main character, was listening to us talk, and he interjected and asked Mama, "Is the ocean like you, Mama? You know how you're always saying you're waiting for us to do the dishes that we dirtied? Is Mother Earth trying to prove a point and make us clean up after ourselves?"

MJ was smart like that. Able to apply everyday life rules to laws of nature.

Malachi: Quinies, Part 4

We live in a city that grew fat on its own filth.

Today, I move through the neighborhood silently, like a cat. Or a skunk, if you ask MJ. I'm coming back from the garden that runs wild and free on the other side of the quiet part of Prospect Park. There are no direct streetlights, so you don't really go there unless you know what you're looking for. I know where to go. I know what I'm doing. I found some berries and greens. But most of it has been snacked on by a group of rabbits I scared away when stepping gently into the green sea of harvest.

When I get home, it's up to MJ to clean them thoroughly with the bucket of water we use to cook with. We have a couple of tins and buckets on the roof that we use to collect rainwater. The pipes were pouring out brown water before we were quarantined, so we're used to having to clean our water. Our landlord earned his nickname, SlummySlumlord, back when he told Mama he wasn't fixing our pipes because we didn't pay as much as the other tenants.

Mama argued, "Stabilized rent is the city's obligation to preserve the community."

She challenged, "If you don't want the tax breaks, or to receive another citation, you better fix my bathroom. Or you will be sorry."

She was the queen of threats. Had 311 and the Housing Authority on speed dial. But that was so long ago. The threats have all vaporized into thick air, and there is no sign of anything getting fixed. Ever. It all feels like a dream.

We turn to the bucket, the small glory of clean water, sparingly. Whatever we don't cook with (using the hot plate I found in the closet from the time Mama and Slummy had a three-month standoff over a broken stove) we use to wash our faces and hands. Our little sister, Lil'Monti, who just turned seven years old, keeps watch for me in the small, exposed, fist-sized hole in the window. When it's nighttime, we patch the window with cardboard and balance old textbooks against it, in case anything or anyone is brave enough to try to ascend the booby-trapped fire escape in search of a new home.

Lil'Monti is small and holds her inhaler in her fist like a weapon. When the virus first hit the city, Mama was afraid. She said, "Monti can barely breathe as is," so we all had to be extremely careful. Washing our hands every hour. Leaving our outside shoes at the mouth of the door. Spraying down the door handles and light switches with disinfectant. Lil'Monti holds her inhaler like a weapon because every time she lost it before, the whole house had to join in on the party. And at first I thought it was the worst kind of party. There was no punch with sherbet swimming in a crystal bowl. There wasn't any music with a DJ to bother with requests to play the "Cha Cha Slide." On this day, Monti holds her inhaler in her left hand, because that's the same hand that held on to Mama.

Now it's just us three: Lil'Monti, MJ, and me, Malachi.

One day Mama and Lil'Monti's daddy, Big Monty, went to look for an inhaler. And they never came back. I didn't care about Big Monty being gone. He was barely "here" when he was present, you know what I mean? And he wasn't the nicest to us, but he wasn't mean. It's like kids got in his way, even his own daughter. That's why Lil'Monti holds on to us for dear life. We are all she's ever known. I fed her bottles when Mama had to work. And MJ let her sleep foot to toe in his bed. Even if she wet herself at night. Even if she woke up crying for Mama.

But I guess Mama loved Big Monty. He was there whenever she needed him, at least for a while. And because Mama loved him, MJ and I tolerated him. Weeks after we waited all night for them to return, only Mama came home that night. Right when the sun was starting to cook. She said she picked up a second shift at the plant and we needed what overtime could provide. But Big Monty ain't come back, at least not that night.

That's before we had a fist-sized hole in the window. That's when the neighborhood was still recognizable. Today, our TV is basically a noise machine. It holds only the sound of static. Luckily the radio signal works in the cassette player, the same one Big Monty used to keep close to his ear. Now we only listen for a change of scenery.

None of the channels play music, just some weird sounds, buzzing and crackling and then a man's voice who urges everyone to "Stay Home. Stay Safe." Stupid slogan ain't changed in two years. And honestly, I hate to tell him—no one even listened to him!

I mean, even if the TV wasn't busted, we probably wouldn't use it. It was broken during a fight between Mama and Big Monty. And if you thought I didn't like him before, I got even worse. I feel like he ain't nothing to me. So I told him so. Mama got in the way of us that summer. But not the fall. The heat had boiled over and so had my temper. I was sixteen going on grown, and he wouldn't move to let me pass him in the hallway. I shoulder-checked him for breaking Mama's TV. I shoulder-checked him for being a bad father to Lil'Monti. I shoulder-checked him for making Mama cry in the shower. I shoulder-checked him for being there instead of my daddy.

I reminded him, "You're not my father. You cap for a living. You cheat for fun. You ain't nobody. You ain't nobody to me."

And then we tussled. He knocked me clean in my jaw. I tried to give him an uppercut like I learned at the Police Athletic League. He grunted, but he recovered, and the next thing I knew, I was on my back, and he was out the door. I cleaned the blood leaking from my mouth. I said sorry to Mama, who was holding Lil'Monti. They both were crying. I'm just glad MJ was in his room somewhere, probably playing *Fortnite*. If he would've hurt MJ, that would've been it. Lil'Monti screamed for me with her hands out. She was so small because of the asthma. I don't like Big Monty, but I'm glad he gave us Lil'Monti.

Our daddy is in prison. Been there ever since I can remember. I used to visit him twice a year. For his birthday and for Thanksgiving. My father isn't militant. He's for the people. He told me to say that whenever someone tried to call him anything but righteous. The newspaper clippings under my bed, the same ones that became window coverings, say he is a part of a group of protesters who are tired of the rich folks stealing from working-class citizens. The newspaper wrote about him sleeping in a city of tents full of humans, all smelling like fruit gone bad, all demanding the so-called gods of Gold Street repay the victims of white-collar crimes: the janitors and small-business owners and teachers and social workers and public transit workers. But the newspapers never seemed to write enough about the Ponzi scammers who robbed all the unsuspecting folks who invested in community buyback programs and one-of-a-kind island music festivals—all pyramid schemes that would leave their pockets empty empty.

Our daddy, Maseo Sr., would give a speech every day. Short, sweet, and to the point. The crowd would repeat what he said and chant it back into the sky. They named it Call-and-Response.

Call-and-Response is when a statement is quickly answered by a statement. It usually sounds like a lullaby, but really, it's revolutionary. Think about it. How many times have you asked strangers a question, and they respond back, clear and present? Not often, right?

Daddy used to say, "Keep it short and sweet, and everybody will join. That's how we get liberation. Everybody has to work towards a common goal. We all got to move to the beat of freedom."

People started to mobilize. They wrote banners and toted them in front of buildings in the Financial District, during lunch meetings by Battery Park, and blocked the bridges from Manhattan to Brooklyn every week. People wrote down lines from his speeches and printed them on T-shirts, tote bags, and coffee cup holders (little-known fact: Did you know they were called zarfs?), and somehow, in time, the lines got a new name: POETRY.

Daddy's words became blown-up posters covered on the glass windows of fancy cafés near Gold Street, and one day a famous muralist, PanoRamo, wheat-pasted it to the side of the wall, and a bookstore near the edge of Wall Street and Chinatown, and that bull statue (yes! Even there too), and on bus side advertisements. It was wild!

On this day, when the weather and the people's temperature had finally reached their boiling point, some irritated person from the opposite side of the protest pushed another irritated person. And all of a sudden, the fight turned into a massacre. The tents were set on fire. And the oligarchs rushed in from the sidelines to blame Daddy's words for inciting a riot. He's been locked up on Rikers Island ever since.

Rikers is made up of ten different jails, and so-called offenders are placed there to await trial, or those serving a term of one year or less. But that's not true. Daddy has been there awaiting trial for four years. They keep postponing and adjourning his case. Because he's so good at writing and talking to the people, they keep him in the SHU. We learned that that one time Mama forgot to get the letter from the mail before we did.

At the age of ten, I was reading anything and everything the librarian at the Grand Army library gave me. Periodic tables. Anatomy books for high schoolers. You name it—I read it. I could read two grades above my level when I was in kindergarten and loved watching *Bill Nye the Science Guy.* Science rules! Which was something to be proud of, except I was bent on reading anything I could get my hands on. Including Mama's mail. Usually, she let me read her junk mail, and would instruct me whether to keep the mail for correspondence or trash.

I saw Daddy's handwriting and I carefully opened the penciled addressed envelope. I was reading the words of Daddy's letter as MJ sat next to me, and it was all about us, "the boys," and we giggled at the idea of Daddy thinking and writing about us. But then the words got a bit harder to pronounce, *post-pone-ment, ad-journ-ment,* and *Secure Housing Unit,* known as the SHU. I sounded out the word, *SHOOOOO.* Said it long sided, like I was talking to a fly. And MJ loved to sing. He pulled his thumb out of his mouth and sang it loud and clear, waking Mama from her nap. I was still reading and my eyes began to leak salty tears as I realized what Daddy was writing.

They keep me in a box. It ain't fit for a human. Six by eight feet and twenty-two hours a day. I don't get a daily shower. I'm lucky if I get a shower once a week. And the food is served cold with a side of moldy bread. The guards laugh at me like I am a joke. I tell them laugh all they want—I'm going to get the last one. I am sending this letter to you on paper I bought with cigarettes. They take away everything and make me beg like I'm not human. But I am a man. I am your man. I am our children's father. And I will not be silent despite their cruelty. This is how they treated Mandela. This is how they treated Ali. I have to remain strong so our sons will know this world belongs to them too.

I was crying. And MJ is still singing. But then he stopped and said, "Mama, what's wrong?"

That was the last time Mama let me touch the mail. That was the last letter I read from Daddy. A year later, when I started middle school, Mama said she'd met someone at the plant and they'd hit it off. I knew what "hit it off" meant, so I started scowling. I felt like I was too old to cry. But that's a lie. Still, I didn't want to cry in front of MJ, because then he would cry, and Mama would cry, so we would all be crying, and who really has time for that? So I kept my levee strong and nodded.

Mama went to see Daddy once a month, still on Rikers Island. They said it would be a year until his trial, but almost half a decade later and nothing. Mama said it was harder and harder to get to see him. Then she just sent letters and pictures from our school graduations. Sometimes we would get a handmade card, but it was always ripped in a corner or taped back together and weeks, sometimes even months, late.

Then it all stopped. Mama talking about Daddy. Daddy sending letters. And I blame Big Monty. I didn't blame him for them punishing my father for something that had yet to be proven, but I resented Big Monty for taking Mama's attention away from Daddy.

I didn't like Big Monty on sight. He was kind of skinny with a tall frame and didn't have any style. I remember Daddy with his camouflage army jacket with the Pan-African flag on the right arm. He wore a red beret and kept his facial hair trimmed and neat. Big Monty wore a mechanic jumpsuit with torn-up construction boots and forgot to take his dirty shoes off all the time. Tracking the mud down our hallway and apologizing when Mama reminded him, as she mopped up the floor.

One day, a year into Big Monty and Mama's relationship, as MJ prepared for a school dance, Big Monty said, "Ain't nobody gonna dance with you if you keep sucking your thumb."

MJ only sucked his thumb when he was nervous or working on a difficult math equation. I tugged MJ's elbow as we sat at the kitchen table. We both turned our backs to Big Monty and refused to talk to him again. We unified like that. Just like Daddy taught us.

I think that hurt Big Monty a little. But he didn't make sense to me. And honestly, until Mama got pregnant with Lil'Monti, Mama didn't make sense to me either. She said she would always love Daddy, but he was gone for a long time and she had to move on with her life. Mama said she didn't like the smell of lonely. I think I was fourteen or so when she said that, and I didn't know what that meant, at least not until now.

Today, Monti, who tells us not to call her Lil'Monti anymore, opens the house door for me.

I go through the ritual of moving silently through the booby-trapped front door.
I inch past the spikes, undetectable to an unknowing eye, in the

vestibule, and finally wipe the sweat from my forehead with the back of my sleeve. I turn the rusted key into the door handle and push into our two-bedroom pre-war apartment. After walking up five flights of stairs, I can't help but release a sound.

I smile and say, "Whoosh."

I know MJ and Monti can't see my smile with this KN95 mask on my face, but I hope my eyes can tell them the truth.

"What's that sound?" Monti asks.
"That's the sound of smiling," MJ answers.

I walk into the bathroom to take off the contaminated clothes and to sanitize my masks and gloves before we eat. I remove the old camo jacket I found in the locker from the hallway closet, and I spray the jacket and the gloves with homemade disinfectant (ingredients include normal household items: two cups of rubbing alcohol, one cup of water, and fifteen drops of homemade eucalyptus oil—from our very own eucalyptus plant). I am ready to go prepare dinner as I wash my hands with the bucket water and a Pyrex glass, but when I look in the mirror, my father's reflection stares back. I am so stunned by my own sight. I begin to weep loudly. Tears pour into the sink as my eyes overflow for the first time in a long time. I sound just like my mother.

Since this pandemic began, we started to count what we really need and what is taking up space or, better yet, can be sold for things we need more of—like food and medicine. So we don't have a lot of things.

We don't have a lot of space either. But we got each other. Blankets, bags of all kinds of potatoes from the urban farm.

"Found it!" Monti yells from under the bed in our shared room.

And I suck my teeth, turn my back to the rescue mission, and jam the pods in my ears. We each got our own phones, but we share the plug. I broke one of the cords. And Mama said something about not being an ATM (which didn't make sense to me, because really, I just need an electronics store or a Dollar Dollar Bargain Barn) and I can fix it. I can fix anything. I turned my old computer into a fan. I turned a battery and rubber bands into a toy for Monti. But I let her think I am listening and turn my phone back on to InstaSnap and watch the live DJ broadcast by D-Nice.

"He's from my time," Mama said, and hooked my phone up to the plug-in speakers.

We danced that night. Monti, Mama, and even I jumped up. MJ came in and watched us, like we were too odd to join. His thumb twitching to give him peace of mind, but his memory always aware of Big Monty's warning. Instead of joining us, MJ went into the room and shut the door loudly. Mama laughed with us, and for the first time, she didn't chase after MJ. The same way she didn't keep looking the streets for Big Monty.

"Your choice, MJ. This is my song!" Mama squealed. And the living room floor became a dance floor. She spun Monti and me using her left and right hands. I took the lead, grabbed Mama's waist, before I dipped her. Monti yelped a surprise, and we all laughed as we fell on the couch.

This was back when we still had a glimmer of hope. School was only out for a week or two, we still could feel the weight of hope in our pockets. Big Monty hadn't returned in a while. Which was unusual because Mama always went looking for him. But I hoped she would stop looking for him and just focus on us kids. Who keeps searching for someone that doesn't want to be found?

I wanted to ask her about Daddy. But those news reports said: The most impacted worst by the virus were incarcerated. And I couldn't bear to hear what might have happened to him. The letters stopped completely after Mama returned, belly-first, home from Rikers Island.

The news said,[1] "America's response to COVID-19 in prisons and jails was a failure."
The news said, "Women's prison and jail populations, and incarceration rates, dropped by a larger percentage than men's populations did."
The news said, "Many police departments were encouraged to

---

1   prisonpolicy.org/virus

use arrest as 'a tool of last resort,' reducing stops, shifting to citations in lieu of arrest."
The news never said anything about our father.

I wanted to know where he was and if he was okay. I wanted the shelter-in-place to be over so we could go back to school. At school, I didn't have to think about anything that brought on the sadness. A sadness so big it would cover my entire body as soon as I walked in our house. A sadness that refused to leave me, even as I slept. It's the kind of sadness that makes your eyes the single truth, and everything else about you is a lie.

That's why in that moment as we laughed and two-stepped in the living room with Mama, her eyes the same pool of melancholy as mine, I let my smile warm the room. I lifted (then) Lil'Monti to the ceiling and twirled as Mama sat on the couch tapping her chest. Like her heart was racing joy with a horsepower she couldn't control. She jumped to her feet, like she couldn't stand to miss the last beat of "her" song. And at that moment, as we danced wildly, the Wi-Fi still worked, everyone who mattered was under this roof together, while the world was on fire and life was still possible, and easy, like water.

Ms. Buchanon: Concerned About Malachi Craig

From: Anita.Buchanon@stellarwilliamsonacademy.edu

To: Symone.Ellsworth.parentmail@stellarwilliamsonacademy.edu

Subject: Update on Malachi Craig

Dear Mrs. Ellsworth,

I am writing you because I am concerned about your son, Malachi Craig. The young people at Stellar Williamson Academy have been deeply affected by the pandemic, and the fear it has instilled in many of our community members has permeated our daily lives. On top of a pandemic, we can imagine how difficult it must be to acclimate to boarding school life for the first time.

There are bouts of sleeplessness or anxiety of fitting in, homesickness, survivor's remorse, and students who fall dangerously into the shadows. So it is pleasing to see Malachi rise above most of the fray. But the concern that I mentioned during Virtual Parents Week . . . well, Malachi is at it again.

Full-on costume for doom, your son! It seems he has a penchant for writing stories about the pandemic taking over all humanity, and well, it's a little frightening. We love his excitement for Mr. Pichinino's creative writing class, but I'm afraid his social skills are not developing as much as we would have hoped. Malachi is a smart and kind young man, but his isolation spells have only grown longer, and he's taken to writing in full costume during the day and sleepwalking in the outdoor garden at night. The final straw was his latest midnight stroll, which resulted in mud tracks throughout the dorm room, which scared Phillip, his roommate, half to death! Unfortunately, this behavior warranted a demerit and verbal warning before Phillip's parents (who are major donors) transferred him to a private room.

I know Malachi survived some scary moments in the city, but I believe we have to get back to normal as quickly as possible, don't you? Here at Stellar Williamson Academy we value privacy and respect for one another's safe space. And it is up to the parents to make sure their child's mental capacity can meet the demands of our school. If this should happen again, we should talk with a therapist about medication. I am available on weekdays between 11am and 3pm if you would like to talk. We look forward to supporting Malachi as he reaches his potential. Won't you help us?

Ms. Anita Buchanon
Dean of Students / Mental Health Counselor
Stellar Williamson Academy

Malachi: Quinies,
an Epistolary Epilogue

Mama,

   Do you want to know why I wrote that story?
Why I share what the teacher from this sterile
boarding school called an Armageddon story? Do you
want to understand why I'm sad? We have all lost
the last three years of our lives in this maze of
worry and fear. I am afraid, Mama, and I am sad.
I am tired of hiding it because it might make others
sad. I am tired of having to hide it in plain sight.
   Being here is not all it's cracked up to be.
Because sometimes I don't even know if these people
were affected like we were. One student in the school
support group says she lost her grandmother. And
two students say they lost their nannies. Another
student with spiky hair and tattoos on their face
says they used to think death was cool until they
crawled away from a house full of dying. They were

saying their parents were getting a divorce after realizing how they didn't like one another. I want to tell the group my little sister lost her father. But that's too complicated. So I only tell the group we lost my aunt.

I don't reveal she is my family by friendship, not blood. By choice, not proximity. They wouldn't get it. They as in these people with family trees that are rooted in slavery and stolen soil. These people that disregard me when I pass them on the way to the library and whisper "affirmative action" or "scholarship" but never my name. They don't even look me in the face when I have to tutor them in chemistry.

You want to know why I wrote that story? It's because I hate that I didn't fight to see Daddy. I feel weird calling him that. I'm almost eighteen and just want my father. I hate that I didn't ask you about our father. What he liked and where he was going.

How to get in touch with him and if we could ride the Q100 with you. I know you said he didn't want us to see him like that, but I can't believe he didn't want to see us at all.

I don't blame you. You lost both men you loved. You blamed their going on the virus. You blamed their absence on the prison system. You blamed the mental health system and the government.

And then you gave me no choice but to leave. You said boarding school four hours away in a car was

Like a field trip to the Bronx Museum and back. You said I would see you once a month.

It's been half a year. I miss Monti and MJ, bad. Even though MJ is still upset with me and refuses to come to the phone when I ring the landline, I miss you and the times we danced in the living room. I don't want to be here, but I know it's the only way forward. I know I will graduate at the top of my class because you didn't raise no fool. But my father didn't raise no liars, so I am writing you to tell you the truth.

The day you took a triple shift at the 69-year-old beer plant, back before the virus shuttered the doors for an entire year and laid you off, you reminded me that you were on your way home and to take the chicken breasts out of the freezer. I had forgotten you told me the night before, too busy with a marathon of Fortnite, and clanged the chains, missing my three-pointer like a beginner. But I couldn't be bothered and called game as I ran home from the basketball courts over in the Parade Grounds. I didn't want to leave it up to Big Monty, who was never dependable, and besides, you left me in charge, Mama. And I take my job seriously. I wanted to get everything done for you, because you do so much for us. I didn't want to smell like "outside," which is just your kind way of saying "stank," and I forgot to lock the front door with the chain (like you drilled in our heads). But I was in a rush to walk MJ & Monti home from Auntie Akeena's. I pulled the chicken out of the freezer and filled the kitchen sink with room-temperature water before stopping the drain with a dishrag. I jumped in the shower for a total of five minutes, tops!

So when I heard the front door handle open and close softly, I dressed quickly and peeked from me and MJ's shared room. Just in time to see Big Monty stuffing the frozen food from the freezer into a dripping plastic bag, juggling my old iPad, MJ's thrift store Js, and your jewelry box in his hands. He even grabbed the chicken breasts from the sink and the rag that was clogging the drain. His hands, Mama, spilled all your dreams onto the kitchen floor, and he didn't even know I was there until I yelled, "YO!"

And for a second Big Monty's shoulders tensed. He turned around slowly from the freezer and almost dropped the items from his arms. He was wearing the nastiest stained white T-shirt that had more dirt marks than its original color and his pants were gummy, like he worked in the oil refinery that day. His hair was disheveled, his eyes were saggy and blurred, his mouth trembled, but he didn't. He was like a zombie. The veins in his arms were bruised, some purple and some black. Sunken moons were above his cheekbones, and his slack mouth moved as he tried to say something. Nothing but a moan came out. And then he cried but he never let go of the stolen goods in his arms. He just held it all to his chest and moaned as his smaller-than-usual frame quaked. Beneath all the dirt and my disgust, I could see he was too far gone.

So I said, "Go on."

I said it so quiet I wasn't sure he heard me through his wails. I just wanted him to leave, Mama—I didn't want him to hurt you, no, hurt US anymore. You worked too hard for us to exist in a city that tried to squeeze the fun and life out of every free and fun thing every chance it got. MetroCard prices surged, tolls were raised, nothing was fixed but everything sure cost more. I didn't realize until I got to this school that boiling water for a bath or heating the house with the stove door open was common, but not normal. And I couldn't stand to see you deal with this letdown too.

I told him, "You can take it. Just leave the chicken." I nodded to the wet stain seeping through the plastic bag painting his T-shirt see-through against his chest.

I told him, "You can go. But you can't take our dinner too."

He walked to the door, set down the defrosting chicken package on the hallway shoe stand, and closed the door as he left once and for all.

He was gone, Mama. But I said it again—louder, so I could hear it too, I guess. "GO!" I said it so I could hear what he heard. My voice deep, cold, and on the verge of cracking into tears. I knew you was gonna be heartbroken, that's why I couldn't tell you. That's why I lied about MJ. I could've left those shoes anywhere, but I told him the truth when we were alone that night. I vowed him to secrecy. When Auntie Akeena offered for us to move in, that's why I agreed to boarding school. That's why I left you to wonder where Big Monty was all this time. That's why I slammed the door on the way out and haven't been back.

But talking to the school therapist about grief, and loss, I realized this sadness may never leave, but I can make room for it. However, I can't fully live if I'm not honest with you. That's why I wrote the story, Mama.

Remember when Auntie Akeena asked you to move in and you almost said no? Remember you went looking for Big Monty, even though you were scared to walk the growing ice trucks full of dead people to go look for him at the hospital on DeKalb, the methadone clinic on Fulton, and the intake center on Troy? That's when I knew, if you didn't live with Auntie Akeena, you would never be at peace. So when the scholarship came, I jumped at the chance. I didn't want to leave you to handle it yourself, but I

knew if you stayed in the co-op Auntie Akeena owned,
you would finally find safe space. And then maybe we
could all find a way through this sadness.

All of us could not live in that two-and-a-
half-bedroom. Even if she turned the living room
into a "players' den" (is that what she called it?),
we would be so on top of one another. And the
pandemic would feel like a cakewalk in comparison.
Maybe not a cakewalk, but definitely easier. I didn't
want the food to grow slim again. I didn't want the
water to run out. I didn't want to watch you stretch
food and resources when you thought we weren't
looking. I didn't want to be the reason you worried.

"You love chemistry," you said.

And you are right. But I loved you more.

When you said, "You going to school is going to
help me more than you know. I love you so much and
I'mma miss you more than you know. You're my first.
You're my sun, son. But I need you to see some more
world before they tear it all up. You can come home
anytime you want. It's an easy train ride—it's just
like visiting the Bronx for the day! We are going
to stay here. Auntie Akeena left the apartment and
even though this place can hold all of us until I
land on my feet—I won't be able to forgive myself
if you don't get to experience your last years in high
school really learning, you know?"

I didn't answer you, but I understood. Even if I

couldn't find the words to talk about it. Even if I never got the chance to tell you the entire truth, I understood.

Have you heard about Aesop, Mama? He was a Greek slave who told fables as an oral tradition and is known as the "godfather" of fables. He wrote about plants and animals with human characteristics. He was an observer that shone stories in hopes of changing our views on the world and when relating to each other.

That is what I am doing here. Observing everyone around me and trying to make sense of tomorrow. I am at the boarding school studying with kids my age who have totally different lives. They are students of wealthy parents who can afford to send them away from the city, whenever they choose, just so they can have the space to learn and live in a safe place. Sometimes they invite me to their vacation homes in Massachusetts, Connecticut, and Upstate, but I don't accept their offers, Mama. I feel like it's genuine, but mostly, I feel on display. I'm front and center for all photo shoots, and even among the beautiful landscape of green and autumn-turning leaves, still, we are not safe from racism here.

Through the week, we all sit at the breakfast, lunch, and dinner tables and talk about the food as if that's the only thing worth being homesick for. But I miss my family. I am homesick for our laughter and dance-offs. I am homesick for MJ's quiet demeanor and Monti's bright bright smile. MJ's earnest eyes look at the camera, his thumb tucked firmly in his small jean pocket, and you on the other side of the camera, keeping them centered in the frame—I'm homesick for you all. But I sit at the circular wooden cafeteria tables and nod mutely as my classmates whine as if the world hasn't changed right beneath our noses.

Can I tell you a secret? I haven't told anyone, not even the school therapist. I figure only you would know what this all means.

You know the night you called me, to tell me Auntie Akeena passed from her lupus complications. How she couldn't find a donor for bone marrow transplantation?

I was in my single room at the boarding school (every junior and senior received their own living quarters and shared the common space like we were in summer camp) where we weren't allowed to have candles in our room unless we were prepared for the monetary fine. Each fine came with a write-up being placed in your file, and after five warnings and fines, you could be expelled. One girl even got her incense taken when the fire marshal administered a surprise inspection at our dorm. You know the night you called me to tell me Auntie Akeena was finally at peace? I missed Auntie Akeena so intensely that I thought of all the things she used to tell us when you had to work through the night. The same nights her limbs were too swollen for her to walk across the parkway to our house and sit with us. Auntie Akeena told us to light a candle and put it in the windowsill to light the way for you to make it back home.

I lit the candle and said everything I wish I could say to Auntie Akeena when she was here. I didn't care about the fine I would incur or the fact that I had zero dollars in my student account to pay for it. Not after the chemistry set and extra books for lab. I lit the candle and thanked Auntie Akeena for loving us and protecting us. I thanked her for getting me my first science kit and for being your sister by choice. And when you told me she named you as her beneficiary in her will, I thanked her for keeping our family safe. I didn't realize I was crying with my eyes closed, I didn't even realize how long I was sitting on the floor, in front of the window, with the darkness creeping closer from the outside of the pane. I got up to stretch my legs, and just before I turned to click alive the light switch on the wall, a loud whoosh from the other side of the window blew the candle out.

It was like a big, sweet breath of air, Mama. I swear I could still smell gardenias after the whole room went dark.

Chorus: Zombie Apocalypse

I ran down the street and saw it all, the flood, the fire, and the zombies!

No zombie neva di deh!

Electra, what do you mean? Don't you remember the outpatient hospital on Fulton? The needle exchange program that turned houses into morgues? Don't you remember we went to Times Square during the fifth week of March? It was so empty it looked like a movie set.

Den mi nuh mus memba?!!!

Nothing moving. No one laughing. No one selling hot dogs or expensive and un-unique T-shirts. Nothing but 11,600 feet of concrete reflecting the sweet soda brand's logo, stark against the night sky. Do you remember the night was so dark, and the blanket silence was so loud . . . I was so scared, but you never let my gloved hand go. Even though everything around us blared "No Touching" and "Social Distance." COVID took so much from everyone and made us all feel so small and insignificant.

We likkle but wi tallawah.

Tariq: Seven Stages of Quarantine

Stage 1 of quarantine, and no one on South Portland and Fulton Street is sure if tomorrow, and every tomorrow thereafter, will be different.

During Stage 1 of the quarantine, the wind is still sweet with spring air and the Brooklyn squirrels have more patience than its politicians.

During Stage 1 of the quarantine, people forget to stay 6 feet away from everyone they may love. During Stage 1 of the quarantine, people hold doors open with a foot planted against its closing, and people wear their masks and sunglasses and latex gloves.

During Stage 1 of the quarantine, people hoard water.

During Stage 1 of the quarantine, people say good morning.

During Stage 1 of the quarantine, people still curse the barista if their coffee isn't made correctly. During Stage 1 of the quarantine, people haven't found the meaning of soft life.

During Stage 1 of the quarantine, people fuss with their Fitover sunglasses, the kind that can be worn on top of prescription glasses, and people are sour about it. It is contagious.

Stage 2 of the quarantine, and no one thinks about tomorrow. People distance themselves from anyone they do not know and have begun to pour instant coffee like sugar water. People have minimalized all of their living quarters. People have reshelved their canned foods to hoard more food. People have begun to smoke when no one is looking. People take out the bills piling up in the mailboxes and stuff them in the empty drawer in the kitchen. People take a daily walk to the park before winter arrives and blanket anything outdoors and everything green. People pretend the drum circle led by the Black man with the red, black, and green styled sweat suit is entertaining when really, people are counting how many people they have lost to the virus. People whisper the word *virus* when they are talking to their neighbors from their terraces. People don't have a terrace—and they live in a garden-style apartment. People make up stories to keep themselves entertained. People watch the news. People do not watch the news. People refuse to clean anything until they begin to smell their body odor when answering the door for takeout. People do not answer the door when the bell rings. Instead, they ask the delivery person to leave it in front of the steps and make a mad dash as soon as the delivery person is gone. People count their steps from the vestibule door to their front door. People lock and chain their doors. People grab a bottle of water from the five-foot stack of bottled water sitting behind the door. People open their mouths and release *ahhhhhhhhhhh!* as if they are refreshed. As if they have it all under control. Sometimes, people still remember what the day is. Sometimes, they still remember the nicknames they received in first grade.

Stage 3 of the quarantine and the only things outside of the house are remnants of a vibrant and bustling city.

Old bodega sandwich bags and sunflower seed shells sit where the drum circle once was. Some people live with others who are disappearing right before their own eyes. These people haven't left the house in fourteen days. People make a Crock-Pot of meat and vegetable stew every night, so in the morning, food relaxes the fear into thinking death isn't as close as everyone believes it is. Some people are parents. Some people are teens. Some people are toddlers. All the people scream. People are forgetting the world they once belonged to. People are creating a new world within the walls of their apartments. People have stopped looking at the death rates on television. People have stopped reading emails. People have stopped forcing homework down the throats of their children. People are happy to be alive. People are terrified of being alive. People miss the days when going to the playground was an easy and meaningless task. People haven't forgotten the walk to the park. But people are too afraid to leave the house. So, people fall into video games, FaceTime, voice memos, and vision board exercises. (The last one isn't their idea. It's their parents' idea. Or their grandparent's idea. Or their partner's idea. Or something they read on Twitter before they deleted the app altogether.) People no longer want to argue about who is the best forward, because the Brooklyn Nets are such a long-ago dream, it feels silly and childish to reminisce over something that may never come true again.

Sometimes, They have a singular story too. It goes.

They walk to get groceries because their grandmother got lost once, and it took them hours to find her. They walk to get medication alone now, because Grandma Marigold seems to keep getting lost and won't tell them why.

Stage 4 of the pandemic is very similar to dementia.
Their Grandma Marigold used to be a jazz singer, but for the past seven weeks, she just hums and gets lost in her neighborhood of the last thirty-five years. They know about dementia because they looked up their Grandma Marigold's symptoms. They noticed their symptoms after they picked up her meds. They discovered there are young people, just like them, who are going through similar things. They met new friends on the Facebook group Grandparents as Parents, and the winter became less scary, less lonely, less cold.

They learned to make a routine for the morning. They learned to make a routine for lunchtime. They learned to make a routine for the evening. They tried to stick to the schedule for the sake of her memory. They learned to celebrate memory. They pulled out pictures and placed the frames neatly against the wall. They decorated the wall with different tapes they had left over from a classroom presentation over a year ago. They remember it's only been four months in the house and they still have living to do. They remember it has only been four months and they know there is so much more living to do, but nothing feels quite right. They read up on dementia and try not to cry. They still haven't mastered that non-crying part yet.

They walk to the bodega for Grandma Marigold's coffee, and its doors are shuttered. They miss hanging with their best friend, Zamira, who moved across the bridge to Harlem after her parents passed away. There are so many people no longer alive. They shake off the cold with a shrug before walking down the empty road to the next bodega. Closed. Then another block to the next bodega. Closed. Before they finally make it to the grocery store in the middle of the block where a line has formed.

They locate their cell phone and scroll through the message board where other grandkids are being raised by their grandparents with a fleeting memory too. They try to scratch the itchy skin beneath their KN95 mask before remembering the deadly cost of a mistake. They try to forget that their ears are cold and bruised from the mask straps. They keep reading the message board with positive responses and pep talks for a group member who may also be having a hard day managing their grandparents' tantrums over being unable to work the stove for something as seemingly simple as a percolated cup of Cuban coffee. Three people exit before three more customers are allowed in. They know instant coffee is all they can afford with the leftover EBT. They scroll down further to see if anyone might have an encouraging word for a moment like this too.

Stage 5 of the pandemic is when they figure out how to mind the land mines of everyday living.

They have taken down the calendars. They blocked the news and programmed the television to show only Hallmark romantic comedies and game shows. They do this for another two months. They fill the prescription. They make canned goods with sazón and adobo. They dream about pizza but pretend they don't. They wake to the smell of the teapot whistling Grandma Marigold's memories back into her body. They open the window drapes and remember there is nothing to see.

Seven months into pandemic living and they just want to go outside again. They aren't able to attend school with their best friend, Zamira. They can't go to parties in the park. They can't take the train or sneak into a friend's house. They can't pretend this is all a game of hide-and-seek. Not when the only person they had in the world is Grandma Marigold. They can't get her sick. They can't lose her too.

They go to class on Google Meet. They talk with a school counselor on Zoom. They play video games on FaceTime and they never see anyone without a mask in public. They don't worry about Grandma Marigold going sauntering through the neighborhood for coffee anymore. They pick up her meds when she is napping or committed to learning who the winner is on *The Price Is Right*. They laugh at all her jokes but have to remind her when they are in a class session. Sometimes they forget that she doesn't mean to forget, and they are incredibly sad immediately after.

They make it up to Grandma Marigold by remaking a memory she frequently talks about. It's always about her time as a singer in a jazz band. One day, they re-create her favorite lounge in their living room, drape deep-red curtains across the windows, and light the small bodega candles near the entrance. They look for decorations to make the room more alive than unalive. They don't cry when Grandma Marigold wakes from her nap surprised, tears forming in her eyes. They prefer to cry by themselves when they are alone and the emotions won't frighten Grandma Marigold.

They locate an old microphone and plug-in amplifier in the back of Grandma Marigold's closet. They wonder if they can talk her into singing her favorite Billie Holiday song. They remember her talking about Jim Crow, Emmett Till, and the reason "Strange Fruit" was such a necessary pain. They don't rush her to finish the story when she reminds them how she had to run away in the night.

It always begins with her father, a sharecropper, being threatened with a shotgun and noose by the local racist teens. A group of kids who thought a light-skinned Black man shouldn't have all the land and pride he had. She always tells the story like it's the first time. And they let her, waiting patiently for her to finish so they can be alone together with their sadness. Together in a safer place where memory keeping doesn't feel like a blindfolded jaunt through an emotional land mine. They surprise Grandma Marigold with her evening chamomile tea from a twice-used tea bag stored in plastic wrap in the butter drawer of the refrigerator. They realize winter is arriving when the candles near the windowsill extinguish the flicker with a whoosh.

Stage 6 of the pandemic looks a lot like Stage 5.
They think it is because of the re-created blues lounge sitting in the living room. They trick Grandma Marigold with time. They trick time. They trick themselves. They don't go out much anymore. They've focused on the canned foods and the Crock-Pot until the first of every month.

This is the ninth month. This is how they mark time using charcoal on the back of their bedroom door. This is how they celebrate the holidays. This is how they do their homework using charcoal. They make calls to the in-home nurse unit. They found the flyer promoting services for the elderly. They found the paper sticking from the community board when waiting to pay for the usual staples at the grocer. They check the news feed on their phone daily to see how many people have gone ghost to the virus. They check the Twitter feed, daily to count down the days a vaccine will be available for Grandma Marigold. They don't want to upset Grandma Marigold, who has regained some of her mobility.

They love when she remembers songs that play on the television show. They caught her standing next to the microphone the other day. They forgot what day it was, but they will never forget how happy she looked. They call Grandma Marigold Ms. Marigold when she holds her mocktail of Diet Coke topped with two canned cherries in one hand and the microphone in the other. They pretend they misplaced the hammer in the drawer with the spoons. They pretend their phone number is a jingle and wait for Grandma to join in during commercial breaks. They let Grandma Marigold fall asleep without bothering her.

They can't forget the day because Grandma Marigold needs them to remember. They remember to call the nursing aide for assistance every Monday. They are excited when they learn Grandma Marigold is first in line for the vaccine. They watch Grandma wake and ask for her special drink. They watch Grandma Marigold bloom some days and wither on others.

They talk to their friends from the message board. They trade secrets and tips to keep themselves near a smile. They rarely smile, but they dream of smiling again. They tell Zamira entire stories using emojis and shorthand. They register for in-person classes after Grandma Marigold gets her first shot. They tend to her swollen arm and let her sleep the ten hours away. They try to fix their bike when she sleeps. They hide their bike in the closet when she's awake. They go to the grocery store and forget the date. They go to the grocery store and forget the EBT card. They call themselves bad names, and Zamira says, "Be nice to my friend."

They try to be nice but they feel like they are failing. They walk home slow. They walk home fast. They forget their phone number. They forget more than they remember these days. They say the date to themselves twice a day. They ride their bike to make sure the chain is fixed. They fall and rip their yellow jacket on the pothole in the middle of the street. They want to cry, but the anger is too deep. They walk the bike home.

They meet Grandma Marigold at the door. They notice she is dressed in her fancy kaftan, which means she wants an audience. They call her Ms. Marigold when she has on nice clothes, and open the window when the snow begins to melt. They play audience and cheer her on when she sings Nina Simone, and it's easy to forget she is losing her recollection.

They watch Ms. Marigold move like the melting snow into Stage 7 of the pandemic. They watch Ms. Marigold spin her song like a ribbon; they watch how the ribbons spool light across the room. They watch Ms. Marigold, who has inched farther and farther away from their reach. They watch Grandma Marigold and feel the weight in their chest lift as they remember the in-home nurse will arrive next week to help care for her more regularly.

They think, *Look how beautiful Ms. Marigold is, the way she dips her head forward with a slow curtsy, her going memories in one hand, and her diet cola and cherry in the other.*

Chorus: Hello, Stranger

Electra, have you ever thought about all the things you forgot?

Yuh gwine staat early like di rooster?

Serious! I mean, look at Tariq's nana. The pandemic changed her whole life. It's hard enough to deal with memories leaving you in a place where you can't remember what you love the most. But now, not being able to walk the neighborhood or remember the faces where masks now sit.

Real haad. Real bad tuh learn yuh whole world tun upside down, and yuh nuh have no control.

The pandemic made it easy to forget, didn't it? That we have each other to care for and worry about, not just ourselves. Look at Tariq, and you think they were an adult, not a teenager!

Hyacinth, do you ever miss being a teenager?

Sure I do. But the world doesn't make it easy to remain kids, eh? And Tariq is smart. They know they would be a part of this nasty game of Duck, Duck, Goose, if they didn't take care of their nana before the effects of the pandemic damaged their family any more.

Nobody nuh safe.

Why don't adults listen to us? Why do teens have to take care of everything?

Zamira: Foundlings

"A bird in the air means we can still breathe." That is what my sister, Tamara, says. She is older than me by five years, which means she is the boss of everyone. It's always been that way. Even before COVID-19 made us orphans. Tam (only I am allowed to call her Tam) is twenty, which makes me fifteen, which makes her my boss. Anyways, that's what she said when we argued yesterday. Tam was on her way to work. Grocery delivery service in a city of eight million people plus is serious stuff. And she hustles. She even picked up delivery gigs around our old neighborhood.

Tam says, "Never forget where you came from."

Her phone is constantly chirping, and sometimes she works so much that she falls asleep sitting in a chair with her run-down sneakers still on her feet. She wears medical gloves on top of a pair of shiny cheetah-print winter gloves. She wears shiny gloves so when she forgets to be grateful, the sun will hit her hands, and the splintered light will dance everywhere.

Like the stars used to dance in the sky.

"Think about it," I tried to convince Tam. "A cat will help with my anxiety." She just shakes her head, places her KN95 mask over her nose, and slams the door on her way out. It's like she doesn't understand anything but money. But there are more important things than money. Every day I wake up, and I'm at Level 5. Most people wake up at Level 1. But not me; it's like I'm wound up all day, and I haven't even had a bowl of oatmeal yet. This feeling that itches up my arms until everything feels like I've got chicken skin. I tried to tell Tam about it. But it was Mommy who always took care of me, so Tam doesn't really know about the buzzing that happens in my chest every month and spreads through my body.

Over twenty thousand people fled from New York City, and all I have to show for my existence are the meds the doctor ordered. Antidepressants are no joke. If I miss a day, it's like I remember all the sadness I tucked away, and every single item unravels from the closet, just in time for me to try on my heaviest blues from behind my eyes; the blues preen themselves into different shapes. The shapes carry all kinds of tunes and voices. *Intrusive thoughts* is what my therapist calls them. Anxiety reveals itself like a pimple in a mirror. Irritating and ugly and coloring my day the worst possible shade of human.

Therapist says, "Intrusive thoughts are not true. They are shape-shifters, and they are fueled by fear. Fear of what might happen. Fear of what may never happen. But if you take a moment, inhale deep, and remain present in the moment—those intrusive thoughts have nowhere to hide."

Today, we live uptown by St. Nicholas Park. Which is really far from my favorite bodega in Brooklyn, where Pops calls me by name and Pepe always smiles nicely. I never have to tell them what kind of sandwich I want; they just know. But Tam found this apartment during a lottery, you know, where the really important and greedy land developers have to section off housing for lower-income families. So now we live here and I attend hybrid classes at the Uptown Charter, which gives me time to sit in the window and look across the road at the park. I promised Tam I would never go to the park without her. Not ever, which isn't that difficult anymore since COVID came. Curfew became mandatory, and hashtag VaxxWars became the norm. Going outside aimlessly could get you sick or, even worse, kill everything in your path.

I open the orange medical tube and take one pale pink pill with the last of my Pink Ting. Soda in the morning is a no-no, but we've moved anxiety pills from green to pink, and I don't care what's a yes-yes; I want my breath to stop running out when I think about homework or traffic lights confusing me when it's time to meet up with my best friend, Tariq. My eyes roll back into my head like clockwork as I swallow these small moments of peace. When I open my eyes, Tam stands at the kitchen door, eyeing me curiously.

I blink rapidly. "What?"

She removes her face mask. "Squish, did you hear me? I said I'll be back before dinner. Make sure you have the salad ready. I'm bringing rotisserie after my shift."

I am still angry from our earlier argument. "Fine!"

My name is Zamira. But when Tam is trying to be extra disciplined and sweet, she calls me Squish. I earned that name when I squeezed between Daddy and Mommy during their cuddle session on the couch before my bedtime. Tam would come home, shake her head when she saw me, and yell as she went down the hallway, "Go to bed already so they can have a life, Squish!" I guess the name just stuck.

Being upset at the person who saves your life daily is difficult. But it turns out—we can't stop feeling our feelings no matter how much we love someone. And I love my sister; she's the only real thing I have left in this world. Tariq moved in with their grandmother in Brooklyn; I never see them anymore. Not since both parentals are gone.

I'm lonely even though I have plenty to do. We have all kinds of plants in the apartment. We have a garden that grows squash, tomatoes, and a small row of lettuce so we can eat the produce we've grown. Sometimes we have plenty of ripe tomatoes, which Tam and I hate. Mom planted the garden a while back, and even after we moved, we brought Mom's raised garden bed with us—I feel like, it's her last living thing. I mean, besides us.

I make a little brown bag of produce for Tariq and Ms. Marigold. I put them in the fridge to hold them over 'til the next time I see them. I hadn't seen Tariq in so long; the last bag almost went bad. Tam started making tomato, pepper, and mayo sandwiches for lunch. "Nothing can go to waste," she says, which is what I sing to the plants when watering them. When that gets too boring, I change my tune. "I don't want no plants; a plant is a scrub that can't get no love from me," in the tune of a TLC hit.

No matter how much I sing, plants don't talk back to me. I'm here alone all the time. In the beginning, it was just me and Tam. Our parents were both essential workers. First we lost Daddy, an urgent care nurse who picked up late shifts at the Barclays Center in Brooklyn while Mom worked at a hospice facility on Roosevelt Island. They both caught the virus while working, and we lost them pretty quickly after that.

In a couple of weeks, the CDC promises that a vaccine will be available for ages 16 to 64. Sometimes it doesn't even feel like it matters anymore. Both our parents are gone. Fr fr, a large part of me is already gone too.

Tam shakes her head. "I love you no matter what. I just don't think we can afford what a kitten needs right now. I know you are lonely. I am trying my best. But maybe—"

"I know, I know." I interrupt her and begin rinsing out my Pink Ting bottle for the recycling bin. "You don't have to repeat it. You are the only one that works. All I have to do is tend to the garden and do my schoolwork. CHECK!" I throw a thumbs-up sign into the air and grin sarcastically.

"Whatever." She replaces her mask. She pulls her scratched-up goggles above her face and heads to the door. She opens it and closes it quickly before I can even say goodbye.

Her disappearance makes my grin fade quickly, but I finally smile when my phone alert sounds.

"Whatchu doing? Do you want to link up before class? It's been a minute since we've both been at school together."

The black letters swim back and forth across the screen. I squint my eyes, and a giggle escapes my mouth. I have yet to see Tariq in person. I mean, it's a panini, right? Tariq lives with an immuno-compromised elder, and we figured enough people lost their loved ones, so we got to keep each other safe. Even if it means we can't hang out like we used to.

I find my joy still. Look for it in all the wrong places. When cleaning and preening the leaves or singing along to old black-and-white television shows on AMC.

I let my happiness spill everywhere in the form of laughter; the kitchen tiles ricochet my sound between the ceiling and walls for seconds. Today is special. I let the song bouncing off the walls become the theme music for today's adventure.

We've been back to school for the past three months. School is on and off every other week because the virus and its family reunion of variants keep shuttering the doors closed. I have asthma, so Tam doesn't play with me being out all "willy-nilly." She says "willy-nilly" like the comedian from the late-night comedy show I wasn't supposed to be watching—but when the administrators cancel school, it no longer matters that I can't fall asleep. It is what it is. And like normal, I have nowhere to go once the sun rises. I watch anything on the internet streaming sites, really, anything that has a laugh track. I ran out of things to watch after *Family Matters, Living Single, A Different World, This So-Called Life,* and *Degrassi.* "Keep your head up, what? Keep your head up, that's right!"

My memories of my favorite television jingle has me so distracted I jump in surprise when I hear Tariq's voice cut through all the city noise.

"Yoooooo!" Tariq yells from the corner in front of our old middle school. Tariq used to live uptown with their pops but had to move to Brooklyn to live with Grandma Marigold after they transitioned. And now I live in Harlem, so it's like we switched places! But specialized schools in New York City mean commuting from borough to borough is light work. Shoot, I remember a girl once took the LIRR train in with her parents so she could attend Brooklyn Tech (one of the best schools in the city).

Tariq is five-foot-five and reminds me daily that they were once taller than me. As freshmen, we walked into the school auditorium at the same height. And after two and a half semesters during a pandemic, Tariq returned still the same height while I arrived two inches taller.

"Ayyyyyyye," I laugh as I cross the street, following the green signals to safety.

Tariq is wearing a bright yellow North Face. It has a couple of tears, but I only remember how they got the rip on the elbow. It happened when we were shooting our film at the old train yard in Queens and almost got caught by the security dogs. We skipped school that day (the trek from Harlem to Queens ain't no joke) to get the final shot for our short horror sci-fi film. That was back when everything was easy. Our parentals were alive and well, and we were fearless fifth graders.

"I got you something." Tariq finishes locking the bike up before reaching into an oversized pocket and pulling out a grease-stained paper bag.

"Is this what it is?" I squeal. Before I receive an answer, I wrench my gloves off and prepare to stuff Sal's bodega breakfast sandwich (with extra cheddar cheese eggs and Salsalito turkey, thank you very much) right into my face. However, the fear in Tariq's eyes reminds me we are still in a pandemic, and there is no cure.

"I'mma eat this as soon as I get home. Thank you, bestie boo!" I tuck the greasy roll fit for a queen into my messenger bag and almost grab Tariq by the arm like we used to. Then I remember "Six feet."

We elbow-tap and continue walking. The North Face jacket fits Tariq perfectly. It's like it's been waiting to be grown into a perfect fit this whole time. And it's the only thing Tariq has left from their dad.

We are still in a panini, a pandemonium, a pandemic—feel me?

School goes by lightning fast, which doesn't mean much. We're in by 8:15 a.m. and out by noon. Class schedules have two different tracks: morning and afternoon. Tariq's surprise attendance today made me geeked and the day went by in a blink. I haven't laid human eyes, real-time eyes, these brown eyes on my best friend in months. I want to pinch them to see if they are here, here. I want to slap their shoulder and fall into a snortful pile of laughter. But I remember "Six feet."

No high five. No laughter into a hug. No wrestling. Nothing. So strange. Touch is necessary for survival, so mothers nuzzle their young as soon as they're born. Did you know a human needs four hugs a day to survive? And for healthy emotional growth, we need twelve hugs a day! (That's why I need a kitten, but I digress.)

Tariq and I know what a hug can cost. We wear our masks in classrooms. We don't share food or drinks. And we elbow-tap, if absolutely necessary. We love each other too much. Before the pandemic, I loved the city at night. It was an electric shock of red and green, car horns, laughter, and friends dancing on the corners under a streetlight as their spotlight. The air was a fire-cracker life. You could feel the sparks on your tongue without even concentrating. I loved this busy city.

But after the pandemic? You couldn't catch me outside when the streetlights turned on. The once vibrant sounds became scary and dull; the laughter turned into constant tears, and the music went from electronic, house, hip-hop, and reggae to acoustic bal-lads and one lone voice singing from behind an elevated apart-ment terrace. Well, those ballads were actually boss. But still, it's just different.

It will never be New York City perfect again.

Tariq says one day, "You'll rediscover your night owl powers. It takes time, that's all." But I haven't been able to find anything I lost in the pandemic.

When our dads picked up a security shift on the night of the lockdown, Tariq and I were at my house being "babysat" by Tam.

Daddy loved working at the Barclays Center. "I can watch my favorite team, Brooklyn Zoo!" he would sing. Even though we lived uptown, Daddy was a Brooklyn kid. So, when Brooklyn got the Nets and he couldn't afford season tickets, he got the next best thing: a gig there! I'm telling you, he was a fan from the beginning. Back when tickets cost fifteen dollars, the DJ would shout you out from the jumbotron screen if you knew all the dance moves.

Mommy loved him working shifts here and there. She said, "We'll have enough to get a second car in no time!" Tam loved it because she didn't have to pretend she wasn't on the phone with her boo all day. TBH, I loved it the most because Daddy brought home all my heart-desired cheese popcorn!

But that night, while we watched our footage and tried to edit the film on our iPad app, Daddy stopped someone from entering the center. He said they had a cold sweat but no fever. Back then, folks had their temperature screened just to attend the events. This ensured that the event didn't turn into a super-spreader. But the temperature check wasn't foolproof and people lost money and their lives if they weren't careful. Daddy said he checked the man's temperature twice, and nothing registered as off. But from working at an urgent care site, Daddy could tell by looking at someone if they were sick. The man didn't want to leave, because he had season tickets. He made a complaint to head of security at the VIP platinum entrance and tried to get Daddy fired. Put up a real stink while coughing the entire time. Daddy said he didn't want any part of it. Daddy wouldn't let the man in, and when he returned home, he didn't forget to bring a bag of my favorite popcorn. The next day he was back at work like clockwork, and every day after that for the rest of the week.

One day Daddy was irritable, complaining about an itchy throat and night sweats; then a week later, he was in a coma. We weren't allowed to go into our parents' room. He isolated himself like a tomb with a microwave, cans of soup, and water bottles. He never left those four walls, at least not when I was awake. So the last time I got to sit by Daddy was when he brought home the popcorn. I let it go stale, waiting for him to get better. But he never did. And soon Mommy, who tended to Daddy with blue latex gloves and a surgeon's mask, became more tired than usual. Two weeks later Daddy passed away. And in less than a week, Mommy began to wilt too.

I lost my mom, dad, and sister in the pandemic. When my sister became our caretaker, I guess she lost herself too. Tam works every single day, ten hours, easy! She swears we will starve if she takes one day off. I wouldn't know because I haven't missed a day without water, lights, or a meal. It scared me when she yelled at the top of her lungs during our last argument. "You need electricity, right? You like food, right? And you best believe the landlords are still evicting people! No one cares about COVID-19, right? Right? So I need to work."

Which is why I asked for the kitten. I read this cool guide online about calico cats. (Did you know calico cats only refer to the tricolor fur, which can be any cat breed?)

The guide talks about calicos being strong-willed, like Tam. I figured it would help with my loneliness and my anxiety. When Tam is gone, I worry. At least then I would have someone to share my tuna fish sandwiches with. And we don't have to worry about them bringing in germs from outside—because we'd be in the house together. I would make obstacle courses using shoeboxes and play toys from the old fur patches in the front closet. Really, Calli would pay for herself. But Tam refused to listen to me. Either way, I decided I was going to get a cat. I'm fifteen and three-quarters. I can make some grown-up decisions too.

Did you know cats need shots? Have you heard of flutes? And not the instrument kind of flute I learned about in fourth-grade music class. I'm talking about flutes, the illness. It has to do with their urinary tract, and you can't give them cranberry juice or anything. May finally arrived and I still don't have a cat. I have new face masks. I even have new shoes because my size nines became too tight, and oh, did I mention I STILL DON'T HAVE A CAT? I sing this when I am taking care of the plants. The tomatoes grow anyway; it's like Mommy is speaking to me. And Tam still works too many hours. Nothing is different. I miss my best friend, who is literally shrinking right before my eyes during our video call. It's been 14 months of lockdown. That's a "1" and a "4." And to be honest, that's too many months and not enough sitcoms. It's been 8 weeks since we last argued about getting a cat. It's been 6 weeks since I first screamed in the pillow, "I hate this! I'm so lonely!" It's been almost four hundred days since Mommy and Daddy were here. It's been ten thousand two hundred twenty hours since I could breathe easy without fear of The Rona.

Soon, it'll be my sixteenth birthday, and I've decided my sweet sixteen gift to myself is a big ol' shot of the vaccine in my arm. Tariq will meet me at the urgent care in Union Square, where we have already signed up to get our first Moderna-na-na-na shot together. That way, Tariq isn't putting Ms. Marigold at risk and may return to school after the summer. They hate homeschooling but said they found a group of kids online, which makes it less lonely. I get it. Internet isn't my thing, and I hate being home alone.

Okay, so look. I want a cat. Let me tell you why since, obviously, you are the only one who cares. I've wanted one ever since I walked by a calico cat. I read somewhere the characteristics go like this:

1. they are spunky
2. they are independent &
3. they are sassy.

Calico cats are swatty when they feel disrespected. Calico cats stand up for themselves, which I can learn from. I need a calico emotional support pet, so it can teach me how to depend on myself when all I want to do is ball up in a cover under my twin bed and wait for the wind to stop howling. Calli (yes, I have already picked out a name) can teach me to be spunky when I am unsure of what to say. Maybe Calli can teach me to be sassy when all I want to do is cry.

Did you know cats help with our mental health? They reduce anxiety and stress, cure loneliness, and calm your nervous system. You don't even have to walk them!

It's like a potluck of things that make my day almost impossible. Last month I started pacing if Tam wasn't home by 6:15 p.m. New York City in the winter can be scary at night. Did I tell you how night sounds remind me of night creatures? The wind whips against the brick buildings, the trees, and the overgrown branches hold secrets until the sun rises; they all have an eerie sound of their own.

We used to live by Fort Greene Park. I don't remember it, honestly. I was just a baby when Mommy would take me to visit her Columbia college friends in "Mecca." Tam told me back then we could only afford rent in "Medina" because living outside of Brooklyn those days was too expensive to make ends meet and raise two little kids. Our family has only two photo albums: Mecca (what the locals call Harlem) and Medina (what the locals call Brooklyn). And they are filled with grease-stained, tear-struck Polaroid slicks of our time as a family when we all were alive and living in places made famous by art, hip-hop, jazz, and smiles like ours.

Most of Mommy and Daddy's photo albums are of them at a park in Medina. Before I was born and when Tam was little, they used to go to Summit on Top every Sunday. Tam always has to tell me the story of the time she watched old funk bands, young neo-soul singers, and rappers take over the granite stage. Alongside the 33 steps of the Prison Ship Martyrs (a monument built to commemorate almost twelve thousand people lost during the Revolutionary War), Summit on Top became the perfect place for a musical roll call. A sea of people and baby strollers, blankets, old bedsheets, and small handheld charcoal grills lined the green patch surrounding the memorial steps; people swayed like the ships that once embraced death. Photos in the Medina album are creased with laughter. Soda pops and little light spots fill in the frames with people whose hands hold cans of Tabs, Sprites, and ginger beers, oh my!

When I look at the pictures in the Mecca photo album, I know everything there is to know. I know how to walk through the park and miss the poop piles left by the horse and carriage rides. I know how to watch for joggers at a specific time because they run the park like trolls run Twitter. I know which block has the most rats on trash day. I know how to disappear when it all seems too heavy to hold.

But when I look at the pictures in the Medina photo album, it's a time warp. Nothing is familiar, not even our parents' faces. Tam pretty much looks the same, but our parents look so young and undead. There are pictures of people, blankets, tubs with ice and half-empty water bottles, and a DJ set up under some trees.

In all the pictures, my parents are hugging each other. Sometimes, they are holding each other, and Tam is standing with her little hands locked tightly at her waist, peeking at the camera defiantly. But our parents, man, they look so happy. They laugh with their eyes closed, and mouths turned to the sky like they're catching joy from the sun's rays. Whenever I think of those pictures, my heart stops racing so damn fast. It goes from a Golden Gate Fields stallion race to a petting zoo pony trot. If that doesn't work, I sit in the corner of my closet with Mommy's old lavender eye mask (she used to put it over my eyes when I began to overthink my school presentations), and I think of those pictures. Our parents looked like they had a lifetime of dreams tucked neatly behind their smiles, ready to develop.

Chorus: Loneliness Leave Me Alone

Wen yu feel lonely?

When do I feel lonely? That's a good question. I guess like Squish, I feel it when no one listens to me. I feel it growing teeth when I hold the door open for someone else, but they don't say thank you. I feel it when I lie down and look at the sky and think about how many people are no longer here. The streets are all empty, and the sound in the air is full of its heavy.

Heavy like the groceries Tam must get up and down the streets safely, like the—

Mi undastan Squish, more an more.
Tek yuh time. Tek a deep breath before yuh get carry weh!

Electra, they gave us all pills. Some of us didn't walk away from them so lightly. Some of us carried those whale-sized fears on our shoulders until those little pills took away the big world of worries, at least for a little while. Some of us didn't need the world to disappear, but the problems altogether. Some of us didn't need the world to disappear, but the gaslighting of our response to the problems of the world. Some of us didn't need the world to disappear, but a place to feel like we belonged and were heard, ya know? I don't know who I would talk to if I didn't have you, Electra. What about you?

Lonely ebi. Mi feel di weight alla di time.

Marigold: Jazz Is Like

You ever heard a horn squeal?
It sounds like five, six, seven, eight
Complex harmonies until syncopation slippery
    improvisations
Oh
Gardenias are beautiful
But so are Marigolds
Look
Lively, live wire
Bass strings accented by the tap tap tap of a foot foot
    foot
On beat
Create a new beat
Be the beat
Swing low
Shugga
I mean shimmy and shimmy and shimmy
Fix my drink

I like rum and Coke
I like white liquor hot and clean
I like to be loved under the light of a stage
Look at that horn go
Look at that lady soar
You think this is difficult? Falling out of love with a
    feeling so seasick you dip and dip again your hips or
    your head. Falling into the room and into the groove

Jazz is more than swing
Jazz is more than memory
Jazz remembers itself and so we all truly win
Win Win Win
Dadadadadadadadaadadaa
Win Win Win
Lowlowlowlowlowlowlow
Sweeeeeeeeeet serenade of my man who couldn't stay
    gone for long
A serenade of the son I lost to the fire in his chest
It is best if I don't remember all the pain
But the sweeeeeeet serenade of my true heart's affection
Soulful stress reliever
It lies in between the bass strings
It lives in the piano keys
It swallows like a winged bird against the cymbals'
    echoes
Weeeeeeeeeeee
Let me sing about the tear in my stockings

Watch me croon about the rent too high

Listen to my heart break and ache within each swollen sigh

Jazz is a lyric embargo

Jazz is a blue sky after a night terror

Jazz is where I can save you and me me me me me me

    me me

Pops: Sal's

Welcome to Sal's Bodega. The best thing to come out of Yemen since oil and iron. Yeah, *bodega* is a Spanish word, but in New York City, *bodega* means where-you-get-everything-on-your-block-in-one-place.

Pepe is Sal's adopted nephew, he been working the bodega counter since he was in fifth grade. And my name is Pops—keep the grill hot. Look at my grills! Cheese! I got these pearly joints Above Ground Grillz over in the Albee Square Mall. Let me know if you need that hookup with my peoples over there. They work around the clock.

Why do they call me Pops? Nah. Not 'cause I pop off. I'm a nice guy. They call me Pops cause I love Pop-Tarts. But my real name is Mohamed.

So boom, anything you need, let me know. We got a good thing going. We been a part of the neighborhood since before, before. I mean back when Sal, our uncle's best friend, was working twenty hours solid and only took his breaks for prayer. It was my uncle who sent in his workers from the construction crew to relieve him when Pepe was in school. Then, when Sal said he wanted to go back to Yemen, times was hard and he needed to focus on his ailing wife at home, he sold the store to Unc and we been here ever since. That was almost thirteen years ago. Sal was a good guy. He let everybody from the neighborhood sit for a cup of coffee and gave all the young ones like me a place to work when our families migrated from Yemen for the last time.

Aht Aht, be careful with the refrigerator door, Fat Dude is right there. He's the bodega cat. If you go to any bodega in the city—they got a cat. But you know why they got cats? 'Cause the rats in the city are vicious! That's why Fat Dude is a part of the team. If you search in the aisle behind the cat food for toilet paper, you'll see a calico cat, napping right there! You can call her Calli, she belongs to our delivery staff, Tamara, but we are borrowing Calli for another week of pest surveillance, until Tam takes Calli home. Go on and pet them—they don't bite.

But Fat Dude don't play about the fridge. He'll bump up all against anybody if they try to come in here pushing around all our milk cartons. Besides, I already rotated them. We may not look all fancy on the outside, like those new bright organic supermarkets that's been tearing down the local Royal Fried Wings spots and opening up. We don't play that "sell the milk before it spoils," nah. We keep it homegrown here. You know why we don't let the milk go bad here? 'Cause we live here. *Word to the Mutha.* I went to Boys and Girls High School right over on Utica Avenue. So I know what's up. I know good food—that's why I'm the grill master. Get it?

So what kind of sandwich you want? I can make you anything, it's my superpower.

You following that keto diet? I gotchu with the grain-free bread, egg whites, and pepper turkey. Put mayo and mustard just to keep it together and slap that baby on the grill. Sizzle sizzle boom.

You want that bacon-egg-and-cheese. But fancier? We got beef bacon. Turkey bacon. Faking bacon. Nah, we ain't got the pork here, but it tastes heavenly on a kaiser roll, so soft, you mistake the bread for a cloud. Slap on some honey mustard with a fried egg on top, and a dash of hot sauce? Sizzle sizzle boom!

You want fries?
You want macaroni salad?
You want tuna melt with lettuce and tomatoes?

I gotchu. But don't keep that refrigerator door open too long. It's hot out here. The streets it's always hot in this city. You know Jay-Z? That's my guy!
He made that New York anthem, with Alicia Keys on the keys, jeez? It was like the city puffed its chest up and anytime that song is on, it doesn't matter where you are from or what you are going

through, you start singing the lyrics about a concrete jungle. I promise. New York City is magic. Even in the midst of all this mess.

When the pandemic first hit, Pepe and I lived back here. We had to keep the doors locked and serve everyone through the window over there. Yeah, the one by the cigarettes. We sold everything we had at one point. It was bare in here, yo. Just us and the cats, some cat litter, a little bit of canned food, and dassit! Word life.

Times was hard for all of us. The PPP loans didn't come through for everyone. I'm telling you Congress ate good on them loans while all the brothers and sisters in the hood damn near starved. We figured it out though. But it ain't luck. It's the neighborhood. We are family. We don't treat people like animals here. You don't see us following you around stores, nah. We treat each other with respect and kindness. That's on everything I love.

So what you want to order? I can make you anything.
I make the best chopped cheese. Ask anybody.
I make the best chicken cutlet parmigiana hero, someone from Milan, Italy, told me so, so you know it's true. Word.
You don't eat meat, no problem, Akhi. My sister is one of them vegetarians too. I got veggie patties, Impossible patties, soy patties, mushroom burgers, add some peppers and onions—sheesh, you won't know what hit you! And I use the little panini press just for the veggies 'cause we don't cross-contaminate. I told you, I'm the king of this. Call me Pops the Grill King.

You need the Cheerios? Cream of Wheat? Oatmeal? You look like you like trail mix. I got this new organic one that came in. Cranberries and walnuts with local beeswax, for your allergies. I keep the Pop-Tarts next to the other breakfast bars. Right before the Cap'n Crunch, Cinnamon Toast Crunch, Raisin Bran, and Lucky Charms. I keep the milk fresh with alternatives to cow milk, because not everybody can digest whole milk, feel me? So we got almond milk, oat milk, soy milk, rice milk, and cashew milk. We got some of that Carnation milk you stir to life with water. Whatever you need, we got it. And if it ain't here, we'll get it next Tuesday. Raekwon, our delivery guy, brings us the best of the best, feel me, fam?

I call everybody family, even if I've never seen them before, under this sun, because we are all a part of the same family, nahmeen?

I've been here for twenty years. From Yemen but in Bed-Stuy, Brooklyn. You know what they say, "Bed-Stuy Do or Die," right? Word to Biggie. Have you seen his mural over on Fulton and St. James? He got several of them joints, actually. Too bad he wasn't here to see it while he was alive. It's beautiful, yo. But you know what he said about things changing . . . right?

Who, me? I've been working in this exact deli since I was eleven years old. Even after the landlord tried to burn the neighborhood down because he wanted to raise the rent prices. What a joke. Raising rent prices in this economy?

But nah, I been at this store since *before* before. I was going to MS113, so I thought I was going to be a performer or something. Then I got onstage and guess what—stage fright! That shut that down. But I love talking to people. Even when I first arrived and had a thick accent, and people didn't understand what I was saying, it was my classmate Raekwon who stood up for me. He wouldn't let folks pick on me for my accent or my clothes. Raekwon and I played ball right after school over on Troy before Unc called me to the store to pray. Then we would open back the shutters, and I worked the counter until it was time for dinner. I wasn't nothing like I am today. I had to grow into this swag. Nah, for real. I love the business of making people feel like they belong here. That's why I'm so charming, you're welcome. And I know everybody.

True facts, I know everybody. And they mama.

I know Esme wants that grilled cheese with American slices and four beautifully thin-sliced tomatoes. She's a nursing student at Brooklyn College. Too bad COVID made her first year an online experience. But lucky for the hood, because we need nurses at the clinic. She says she studying to make sure the people here ain't forgotten because of the way they left us all here to fend for ourselves when the virus came—it's wild, yo. If it wasn't for Esme, we wouldn't have the clinic working as good as it is. First, they took care of the elderly's houses. We started to run errands. Bringing them their prescriptions from the clinic along with the groceries. We got a cool thing going. Which we needed, because we are essential workers. If we ain't open, where's the meat? Where's the produce? Folks on canes can't walk all the way to downtown for food all the time. And everybody ain't got a whip. The buses weren't necessarily safe, so we started getting double deliveries from Raekwon and made sure everybody had what they needed.

I know Damar needs two sandwiches. One hero and one roll. He always gets one for him and one for his son. Sometimes it's peanut butter and jelly and sometimes it's turkey meatball sub with mozzarella and extra sauce. He used to get three sandwiches, but after the pandemic, his wife passed away from breathing complications. He didn't come in for a while and when he finally came back in months later, I cried. Deadass. On sight. I thought he was gone forever. So many people never came back. Sister Linda, who used to run the after-school reading circle at the park square. My girlfriend's sister, Fatimah. The Reverend Dean from Church Ave. And Damar's wife, Dana.

I know Carrie needs the alfalfa sprouts, cream cheese, on a gluten-free roll. Especially when she's on deadline for her work with the weekly newspaper. She works at the *Brooklyn Rail* and keeps everybody on the block updated. She was one of the first ones rolling up with masks for everybody. Single moms working, the fathers who couldn't afford to take time off or they would lose their pensions from the MTA, essential workers, everybody. She hooked everybody up and then did a whole article about the free masks with a sandwich purchase. She hooked us up, yo! She got Eve to make us a whole social media page. I don't be on the Gram or the TakiTaki like that—but no lie, Eve hooked it up! She made a video and cut it up all nice, like a professional commercial. She said act natural, but I was nervous, right. I got that stage fright when all eyes were on me. But as long as I didn't have to talk, just show off the way I perfected these sandwiches, I was Gucci. She added some fly Brooklyn music to the video and boom! The next thing I knew—we were busy again. The line was mad long. I'm talking down the block! Seems like everybody saw us on their social media and showed up to support us.

We got so busy I couldn't deliver anymore, and Pepe had to work the register. Sal was long gone, and Unc passed away at the top of the year due to cardiac arrest. (The first three days after his passing, we handed out free bread and soup. It's a part of our culture. Then we took him home and laid him to rest.) So we needed as much hands-on help as we could get. Raekwon was moving fresh produce, deli meats, and bagged chips on the regular. He owned his own moving van and didn't have time in his schedule to help us. He was in high demand to transport food from the Amish in PA back to the city.

So we hired Tamara, an old neighbor, to deliver the sandwich orders to the elderly and the clinic. She was good too. Don't tell nobody, but deadass, I got a crush on her. Every time I see her, my heart *badabump badabump,* even when she got her mask and gloves on like she going to space. We don't get to talk as much anymore, she raising her little sister and all. I get it. But she's a dime. For real for real. Anyways, hand to my chest, if Carrie, Eve, and Tamara didn't show up for the hood, nah. Scratch that—if they didn't show up for us—I can't tell you we would still be here. I'm just saying—the PPP loans didn't come through for us, but the hood did.

Anyway, don't get me started. I get sad thinking about it. We are just thankful to still be here. So I make it my business to know who needs what kind of sandwich. It's the least I can do for the people I call family. So as soon as I hear that door open, I know who needs that BLT and who needs the Baconator. Both are amazing sandwiches, if I do say so myself, but the Baconator is my specialty. I designed it with two different kinds of bacon, a soft crusty hero, jalapeño peppers, onions, pepper jack cheese, garlic aioli and deli mustard, oil and vinegar. And pardon me, Pepe, open the door for Fat Dude. Like I was saying, the Baconator is chef's kiss! Deadass.

You ain't from around here? Oh, you new to the block, huh? Where you stay? The brownstone with the garden? Ah, yeah, that was Ms. Ellaine's place? I liked her, she was a nice lady. I heard she moved to live with her children in California, is that true? I know the stairs were hard for her. But when her grandkids visited, she always sent them to us for quarter chips and Capri Suns, or freezee pops and fruit snacks. We kept her running tab open and like clock ticks, she paid it off, every month. But we don't do that for everybody. I mean you look like a nice person. But we had to change that policy a *long* long time ago. Only the elders got that special pass from Sal, the original owner, and he's gone.

So wait, where you coming from? The Motherland or the Midwest? That's cool. I bet you they can't make you a sandwich like this though? I promise, I father this sandwich business, yo. They call me Pops, ask anybody.

Yusef: Six-by-Eight

C-76, or NYC Correctional Institution for Men, was a pandemic before the virus got its street name. If you're looking for a name, you won't find it here. We live in a place where the correctional officers call us by our last names but crown the buildings by naming the structures of stone after the wardens of this wretched compound. As if a fortress of concrete, razor wire, tears, and steel named after you in the new age slave trade is an honor. But the block calls me Diggs.

When I first arrived, I would draw on anything I could get my hands on. Envelopes. Toilet paper. The wall, the sheets. Drawing has always helped me keep my mind mine, you know? Anyway, one person found out, then another, and another. One of the older heads, this revolutionary dude named Maseo Sr., gave me the nickname. I'll bet donuts to the dollar he nicknamed me because he misses his two sons, but I don't mind. I like it, and it stuck. Next thing I knew, everybody was requesting me, Diggs, to create one-of-a-kind handmade cards with sketches

of flowers, people's children, city skylines, and cartoon charac-
ters to send a kite across the water to their loved ones and get
paid. It was my first real job! It's the only job I ever had before
I ended up here.

I've been here for thirty-seven months. I turned eighteen in this
place. The same month the virus shut the whole city down. No
candles. No cake. Just fear of a cough that had the power to shake
your entire body and steal your breath away. At first, there was
nothing different. They shut down visitation hours, which didn't
affect me, but that act to keep us safe ultimately changed the din-
ing hall's temperature for the worse. No one was allowed to leave
the grounds, to make sure the inmates would remain safe from
the virus. But once the correctional officers started filtering in
from the city to begin the twelve-to-fifteen-hour shifts, wet and
deadly coughs covered every inch of the building.

Outside, most of the city had access to soap and hand sanitizer.
No such luck behind these steel bars. When we heard the news
of "shelter in place," it struck some of us with a weird sense of
humor. Is this shelter? "Three hots and a cot?" an older inmate
sang. One cough turned to five. Soap, what a dream. Five coughs
turned to hundreds. Hand sanitizer, who? And in less than two
weeks, we went from one COVID-19 to almost 200 cases of
COVID-19.[2]

---

2   theguardian.com/us-news/2020/apr/01/rikers-island-jail-coronavirus
-public-health-disaster

It took lawyers fighting for us to get the vaccine over a year later. And it's the closest thing to normal, even though Maseo Sr. said, "This kind of life should not be normalized."

Have you ever been looked down on? Or have people doubt you? That's how the world has looked at me since I left G Mama's house. And my quiet nature doesn't mean you can step over, step on, or step to me. So on the day of my birth, in a mental space that should have been happy and hopeful, I was in the mess hall with hundreds of inmates. While waiting in line for breakfast, I lost my cool.

A new inmate walked up and talked to me like he knew me. Like he owned me too.

New Kid: "Yo! I hear they call you Diggs, and you can draw? I'mma need you to draw a picture of my girl. Aight?!"

And when new inmates come in, they sometimes mind their business and try to make a name for themselves. With us finally being able to eat in the cafeteria again after they finally administered the one-shot vaccine, I didn't want beef. But I also couldn't let it go. I was already in a bad mood. Anyway, we got in a tussle because we both felt disrespected. And I wanted him to feel as bad as I thought. So I picked up the tray and just swung at his head. Minutes later, Maseo separated us, my right eye puffy, a lump growing on New Kid's forehead.

New Kid roared, "It's over for you."

I laughed dryly, thinking to myself, *It's been over.* Maseo walked up, put his hands on both of our chests, and said sternly, "Enough." He looked at me square in my eyes. The man who nicknamed me. The closest thing I ever had to a father. His eyes never left mine.

Maseo said plainly, "I'm disappointed in you, Diggs. I know it's your birthday, but that means you got to make grown-up decisions. It may not be fair that you are in here—I know, son, it's not fair. But you can't do this. We are not the animals they want us to believe we are. And we are more than our mistakes."

My one good eye began to water because he was right. I could see my G Mama shaking her head from wherever she was now.

I looked at New Kid, my shoulders slumped, and said, "I apologize, yo."

New Kid's grimaces promise he has more threats to offer, but Maseo Sr. stepped between us and offered a matter-of-fact response. "You don't have to accept it right now. But you are going to have to take it, little brother."

New Kid scoffed. "I ain't your brother, and I ain't got to accept a damn thing!"

Maseo Sr. responded, "You are right. You don't. But I promise you, this only gets harder for us if you hold a grudge. I don't know what occurred, but we respect each other here. I can promise you this, he will never touch you again."

New Kid: "You ain't my daddy! I got a daddy! You can be his damn daddy! But I'm a grown man. On the block, I handle—"

Maseo's growl slices the air. "This is *my* block. Understand?" Maseo Sr. doesn't wait for New Kid to respond but signals the guards watching the whole exchange to join us. They never interrupt Maseo Sr. when he lectures in the hall. And that's what it was, a lecture on how to be better.

Maseo Sr.: "I've been here too long, young one. And I know you are a soldier. I can tell by your fighter's stance. But if you keep going, this will end poorly."

As soon as Maseo Sr. turned his back to both of us, the guards stormed us and threw us on the ground. The cold gray concrete kissed my unbruised cheek, and I closed my eye as they tightened the handcuffs. That's how I spent my birthday in the SHU. Which is just a short word for the inhumane treatment of solitary confinement. Ask anybody: The SHU is where you are isolated so long the depression feels like a vacation. The anxiety is the cherry on top.

I believe they created the SHU to break your spirit. In my head, I tell them: *Too late.*

Lock. Lock. Lock.

Sometimes I watch myself from a safe place up in the corner of the room. How else do you think someone could sit all day in a single cell for twenty hours a day with only a dirty toilet, a leaky sink, a cold steel bed screwed into the wall, and an itchy blanket? You have to keep your mind going, or the isolation will take you from yourself. I gave everything a name. I got used to the bedding. I called them Foldie. I got used to meals. They shoot like a hockey puck through the slot at the bottom of my cell door. I called meals ChowChow. I got used to the small window overlooking a sky that always looked gray through the dinge-splashed window. I called the sky Cummi, short for *cumulous.* Now that I think about it, I never remember it being blue. I even got used to the quiet. But I will never get used to not being able to draw my feelings down. And that's all I've ever had. That's all I've ever known.

Let me set the scene. You got time for my story, right?

You might think people locked up deserve this kind of treatment. But what if you were reminded every single day of the one thing you did wrong when you were too hungry to think clearly? What if you made a mistake on your worst day, and the world never let you forget? I didn't do anything wrong— except be born. My mother passed away during labor, and my father, struck with grief, found a bottle to nurse instead of me sitting alone in my bassinet. One night, he left me to make a run to the liquor store over on Broadway and Myrtle, and during a robbery, he became a casualty. No one knew I was home alone all that time until my paternal grandmother, G Mama, found me in a soiled diaper, nearly suffocating from the blanket covering the bassinet. She told me when they discovered me at home alone, almost five hours later, that I was so silent they were afraid to look.

I've always been alone and quiet.

G Mama raised me until I was 13. She would read to me daily, whether from her Bible, her Harlequin romance, or the daily newspaper. She didn't have a working television (unless you count me holding the antenna ears up by the aluminum foil until my arms grew tired). So reading was our in-home entertainment. Which suited me fine. I loved to listen to her read. She had the most soothing southern voice, the one thing she kept after moving from Louisiana all those years ago. Whatever story she read; I would begin drawing on the clean paper booklet she had sewn together for me using yarn to stitch the handmade journal together.

My own little sketchbook. After each reading and sketching session, G Mama would study my work for the day. If it was a sketch I was proud of, I would tear it from the yarn binding and give it to her with a kiss on the cheek. She would find an open space on the old refrigerator, attach it with a Niagara Falls or New Orleans magnet, and hum as she began preparing dinner for the evening.

The following day, I would sit on the kitchen stool to eat my Raisin Bran and proudly face the appliance turned art gallery.

So when G Mama, a firm believer in eating daily portions of pig feet, smoked collard greens, fried pork chops, and mounds of corned beef hash, passed away in her sleep, I didn't realize she had a heart condition. Not until I was placed in the foster care system and interviewed about her declining health.

Foster care was horrible. I was afraid to cry, afraid to leave my drawings, fearful of all the noise that kept me up at night—which made my falling asleep in class quite easy.

My foster parents would fight like feral alley cats. They pretended to be loving parents whenever the social worker checked in on their growing home of "misfits" (that's what they called us at dinner). I was the fifth foster child to enter their Bushwick home. The red-painted gate separated our front door from the JMZ subway exit, keeping us "misfits" caged in on the stoop.

When I first arrived, my FPs (which I affectionately named Evil 1 and Evil 2) looked at my baggage and said, "I don't know where that big ugly thing will fit!" After G Mama's passing, I was allowed to keep one thing, and I chose her old trunk and used it to carry my valuables. My social worker cleared her throat.

The FPs stammered, "I—I—I mean, we don't have space. But maybe we can find a place for it in the basement?"

After I was left in front of the red gate to drag G Mama's trunk down the basement stairs by myself, one of the FPs threw a box of black plastic bags and ordered, "Get what you need and leave the rest down there."

I grabbed G Mama's picture of us leaving church service on Easter several years back, my underclothes, favorite drawing pencils, sketchbook, and sweat suit. Two days later, I went to the basement to grab a clean T-shirt and socks, and my trunk had been ransacked. Whatever was left became a sleeping nook for three flea-bitten cats, the prized possession of the FPs. I never found the rest of my things, but I didn't care. I had what was most important. But the FPs drove me mad. I have never been in a house so loud and violent.

I was a quiet kid and raised to be respectful. Every Sunday, I went to church with G Mama and sat obediently in the wooden pews. The choir was the only thing that could stir my attention from the handmade sketch pad. I never went to Sunday school. I wanted to hear the stories the other kids talked about, but my fear of abandonment would take over my body within minutes, and all I could think about was: What if G Mama leaves too? So I stayed put. Even though I was quiet—I was still inquisitive.

When I became a ward of the state, the FPs told my social worker that I was too jittery. FP1 and FP2 suggested I start a trial run on Ritalin even though I told them I didn't need it. No one listened. I was prescribed ADHD medication, and even though I never took one pill, I wasn't bothered by it—because I didn't need it. But like clockwork, on the last day of each month, Symphony (the only foster brother, who lived with Evil 1 and Evil 2 the longest) would pick up our meds from the pharmacy on Broadway. After Symphony retrieved his hydrocodone prescription, I collected my Ritalin prescription; we raced home to the FPs to hand over our bounty of orange bottles and back outside to play before the sun went down.

I suspected the FPs had us all on medication and made a lucrative side hustle by selling them to folks on the block. When I turned fifteen, I was a beanstalk. And with all the pills FPs were slinging, I asked for an allowance to buy new underwear and toothbrushes from the pharmacy. I was tired of asking for regular items and being shamed or told I was too entitled.

I cycled through social workers, six in two years, and stopped talking to Evil 1 and Evil 2 completely. It only made the FPs angry. They refused to give me the bare minimum, and honestly, I was tired of asking. When FP1 allowed her favorite cats to soil my bedsheets, when I asked FP2 for a new pair of sneakers, they groaned and acted as if my essential needs were a nuisance. This was the final straw.

Symphony (a fifteen-year-old music lover who suffered from sickle cell anemia and bimonthly bouts in the hospital) was small-statured enough to fit most of the hand-me-downs left over from foster kids passing through. I, however, had outgrown most of the charity's options and had to cross my fingers in hopes of finding pants that fit over my ankles.

I didn't want to be the one no one wanted to sit by in class this year. I was beginning high school and wanted a fresh start. All my other foster sibs (only three of us left after two tumultuous years) wore more stylish, well-fitted clothes. They weren't the newest-looking items, but they were clean. Hyacinth was a Caribbean American fifteen-year-old who visited her family on the weekends and came home with clean clothes every Sunday night.

When one of the FPs tried to look into Hyacinth's bagged items, she stared squarely at them and said, "My auntie lives three blocks away. She will be here to box you up so quick—your head will roll." Hyacinth and her bestie, Electra, are two peas in a pod. When you see one, the other is nearby. And even though Electra doesn't talk to anyone but Hyacinth, she has the death stare that speaks its own language. She's nice enough to me, but Evil 1 and Evil 2 definitely act nervous whenever she waits for Hyacinth on the front step.

Needless to say, they left Hyacinth alone. And then there is Symphony, who suffered bouts of constricted blood cells, countless days of fatigue, and indescribable pain that would take his limbs hostage. His constant struggles with the illness make it impossible for him to live without the care of the FPs and their cats. Symphony has been there the longest, and a part of him believed their care, however demeaning and demanding, was a sort of love too. And then there was me. My pants were usually high-watered. The soles of my shoes were talking out the side, sometimes exposing a dirty sock, and I just shot up like a stinkweed. At least, that's what one of the FPs said. So the community thrift closet was fine, until one day I brought home a bag of bedbug-infested items. I itched for months. The tiny welts that spread across my shoulders, the back of my neck, and my entire back and chest left marks. I was so ashamed. That was seventh grade. And as I prepared to finish my eighth-grade exams and presentations, I decided I would have clean and brand-new everything. I wanted to end the year strong. I wanted to go into ninth grade dressed nice and neat. And I would accomplish that goal, even if I had to steal it.

I remember the day I decided I would take it. I was in the lunchroom and had tired of being the butt of the joke. I didn't care much about the cool kids' table. Symphony, Hyacinth, and I all went to the same school, so even if Symphony missed two weeks here and there during his stints in the hospital, I always felt like someone had my back. Let me tell you—Hyacinth was good about shutting people up when it came to me! But it was short-lived. I figured if I remained quiet, no one would notice me. But they always did. No one wanted to be my partner during chemistry classes, but at least I soared in my art class. I didn't think about my bedbug scars in that clean, colorfully painted studio. I forgot about the pockmarks formed on my wrists. I focused on my creations and the canvas—nothing else distracted me—not even my memories of G Mama.

My art teacher, Ms. Ingram, offered me a pad of cocoa butter and said, "Use this twice a day. Those scars can lighten in time."

Ms. Ingram was the only adult who wasn't related to me by blood that I ever felt truly cared for me. Sometimes, I would daydream she looked just like my mother, if I had ever met her. I thought, *She would be exactly like this!* Dark brown locs pulled back from her face by color swatches of bright fabric, warm eyes, a wax print kimono on top of a long kaftan, matched with a pair of paint-speckled Converse. Her color choice of the day would be my inspiration for the week's art assignment, and she never cringed when I walked near her.

One day, she touched my shoulder and marveled at my drawing of the day. "This is beautiful! Is that me?"

And when I nodded quickly, she replied, "You honor me. Thank you so much, dear Yusef. This is astonishing work. You should definitely put this in your portfolio!"

The day our portfolios were due, we were assigned class presentation times. I was so proud of my artwork and how my vision strengthened and progressed after Ms. Ingram introduced us to Mickalene Thomas, Jacob Lawrence, Bisa Butler, Jean-Michel Basquiat, and Derrick Adams, I signed up to present my portfolio last. I asked the FPs for money to buy a new white shirt, underwear, and off-brand white shoes. They were so furious about my Ritalin prescription being halted (throwing a monkey wrench in their side hustle) that they didn't even let me finish asking, turned the television up in the corner of the hoarder-esque living room full of old magazines, unpacked Amazon boxes, food-stained Tupperware, old newspapers toppling onto each other in a corner, matching armchairs decorated with stained doilies and claws shredding the faux leather, and the distinct ammonia smell of old, soiled cat litter. I never crossed the threshold, certain it was bedbug haven since the FPs were the only ones who didn't have an allergic reaction during one of the largest bedbug infestations in New York City history. I only visited the kitchen, bathroom, and basement, and if I wasn't on the porch listening to Brooklyn pass me by, I drew quietly in my closet-sized bedroom.

FP1: "New clothes? Are you mad!"

FP2: "You must think we are made of money. You aren't happy with all we've given you? We feed you every day, don't we? The lights are on, aren't they? What more do you want?"

FP1: "I told you to tell the people at the school you needed the medication. That's how we were able to buy you Christmas gifts."

I think of the stocking full of penny candies, travel-sized essentials, and airplane socks. My feet were too big for them, so I gave them to Symphony. And Hyacinth, who visited her family frequently, brought back a new pack of colored pencils and a bag of tube socks just for me. She gave Symphony a notepad with music notes on the front because he was a poet. I drew pictures of them each and framed them with two plastic picture frames I found in a forgotten stash in the basement. Symphony wrote us acrostic poems using our names as inspiration.

I didn't want anything but to feel good about my outside, the way I felt about my art. I headed to Albee Square Mall with an empty backpack and my mind made up. I was going to get what I needed once and for all. I thought about all the places I would wear the cool bomber jacket and jeans that fit my tall and lanky shape as I looked at the mannequins. But first, I needed underwear. So I went to Target for white tees, underwear, and a new toothbrush. I stuffed some organic fruit snacks into the pockets, sullied jeans for good measure, and rushed to the exit.

I never made it to Macy's.

Once the FPs got the call, they claimed I was too much to handle and hung up. My social worker, Nameless Number Seven, was on vacation, and because it was a Friday, the courts were closed until Monday. I didn't think I would be locked up all this time for stealing underwear and a toothbrush (oh, and fruit snacks).

Every single day I sit behind these bars, I am reminded that it doesn't matter what you think is fair, and it doesn't matter what you believe you deserve. But there are silver linings everywhere. There is hope in the art I make and in the memories of Ms. Ingram, Hyacinth, and Symphony that keep me company. Whenever I get out of here, I'm never coming back. I got my GED in here. I completed classes and received certification in engineering and woodwork. I also received a certificate for completing the poetry program, knowing it would make Symphony proud.

In this six-by-eight, with my right eye throbbing shut and my stomach growling from hunger, the only thing that matters is how I respond to what is next. I think of Maseo Sr.'s family. The two children he left behind. I wonder if they miss him. I also wonder if they know he is saving my life every day.

When I am at my lowest, I sketch Maseo Sr.'s words on the wall. <u>I AM NOT AN ANIMAL.</u> My name is Yusef. I'm an 18-year-old young man. I am more than my mistake. And despite Rikers Island becoming my purgatory for the last three years, I am *not* an animal.

Symphony: "YUSEF"

A poem by Symphony Jackson

Y You are not what people think
youthful eyes with an old soul

U Understanding and kind. You always think
of others when you draw us the sky

S Strong and silent. Your stance speaks for
itself

E Everyone's eyes can see the truth because
of your talent

F Friend, family, fearless, Yusef. I will follow
you forever. The big brother I never had.

Chorus: Preying on the Weak

I miss Yusef. I still have his picture of us, Electra.

Oh yeah?

Yeah, of course. He's going to be as big as Basquiat one day. If we ever make it out of this pandemic matrix. Symphony still sings his praises. Between the hospital stays and the foster parents from hell, we are lucky Symphony is still here. Despite the fever and chills. Despite the headaches and fatigue. Despite the loss of breath and endless coughs—Symphony is still here. Some of us are still here. Mask up.

Bless up.

Tam: To-Do List

1. Wake up at 5 a.m. for the early morning delivery shift.
   a. If you sleep through this alarm clock, you will regret asking for the extra hours of time-and-a-half pay. The tips are better in the morning anyway; folks who want to get the most out of their day tip double than afternoon deliveries.
2. Turn on the kettle.
3. Brush teeth. Wash face. Dress in black leggings, baggy camo pants, tube socks, a thermal shirt, a button-up flannel shirt, and your favorite Howard University hoodie.
   a. Be glad the shower last night with lavender from Squish's garden coaxed you to sleep.
   b. Be glad you have this sweatshirt as a reminder of your parents' dreams for you to go attend college.

c. Clear your head of the grief when you think about what you could not do before you lost them. Now stop whining. Go!

4. Drink instant coffee: three sugars and one creamer, just like your pa taught you. Look out the window while you drink the coffee and hold this moment for yourself. Remember you deserve a moment too.

   a. Sure, Pops will give you whatever you ask for. But you need to trek from uptown all the way to your old Brooklyn homestead, disguised as a bodega. At the very least, the caffeine will save everyone from your bad attitude. Now—hit the road!

5. Make sure you have on your scarf and vintage Brooklyn Dodgers stadium jacket.

6. Don't forget the hand sanitizer, travel-sized alcohol wipes, house keys, and gloves.

   a. Both pairs of gloves!

7. Unlock your scooter from the front gate at the bottom of the stoop, and tuck the chain lock combo underneath the seat compartment.

8. You are still early enough to beat commuter traffic once you pass the Schomburg Library towards the FDR.

9. Stop by the gas station as soon as you cross over the Brooklyn Bridge.

10. While the gas is pumping, call the house phone and let the phone ring three times so Squish knows it's time to get up for school.
11. If she doesn't call you back, call again to confirm she's up.
12. Smile when your cell phone rings and sing to your little sister: Get up, sleepyhead! Have a good day, I love you.
    a. Don't forget to smile. Squish says she can tell when you are scowling and concerned.
    b. Apply a second coat of tinted lip balm. Put your face mask back on.
13. Make sure the gas cap is firmly returned to its rightful place.
    a. Remember what happened the last time.
14. Take the scenic route to Sal's and post your scooter in front of the loading sign.
15. Say good morning to Pepe before Pops. You don't want to look thirsty.
16. Take the orders waiting for the senior home residents, and ask about the calico cat.
    a. Don't look at Pops too long. You don't want to look thirsty.
    b. Accept the coffee and the promise to take the calico home tonight to Squish.
    c. Good job, big sister.

Social Workers' Haikus
Q&A with their clients

Q. I don't like it here, can you take me home?

Nameless #1 Answers
Try to find your place
in the world—don't fall victim
to the broken husk.

Q. Who are you? Where have you been? Never mind, it
doesn't matter. Why are you here now?

Nameless #2 Answers
I am meant to serve
all the forgotten children
but I can't keep up

Q. You don't know how hard it is to be here? Do you know
what it's like to have no dreams? Why won't you help me?

Nameless #3 Answers

Do I hate this job?

Is the city full of sick?

Yes Yes Yes Yes Yes.

Q. Who is your favorite person? Mine was my G Mama.
Did you have a G Mama? Do you miss her too?

Nameless #4 Answers

The wise should guide youth

to make your ancestors proud

Keep marching forward

Q. I called the number on your card, and no one answered.
Everyone here is coughing and gasping. Symphony still
isn't home. I'm scared because Hyacinth won't pick up
her phone. Why can't you hear my cry?

Nameless #5 Answers

The city is cruel

The sickness is just as bad

I can't find my way

Q. What is it like to forget about kids like me? What is it like
to forget? The sick line the streets and there is no food to
eat, unless I steal it. Why won't you answer your phone?

Nameless #6 Answers

I have thirty kids

sitting in houses alone
The system is broke

Q. I bet you don't even remember my name, huh?

Nameless #7 Answers
I have fifty kids
I've never seen their faces
I'm doing my best

Q. When can I go home? Is there a home to go home to?
When you are stuck in a system that forgets about the
children, who protects us from them? Who protects us
from you? They say we can't get sick, but what if we
can't eat? What if we can't sleep? What if we were in
big trouble before the pandemic sneezed its existence
into the world? Who will give us back our dreams?
Give us back our summer internships, and sunset
bridge walks? Give us back our prom season and
graduation season? Give us back the only person who
ever loved us? The grandparents who became home.
The single parents who became home. The chosen kin
who proved a chronic illness can take away your safest
place on this earth? Can you hear me? Who will clean
this mess if teens are always told to mind their place?
Who will clean up this mess if we are always told we
don't understand? Who will feed us soup and lullabies
until we feel whole?

Nameless #8 Answers

. . .

. . .

. . .

Q. I'm sorry, I'm sorry. Just one more question. Will the world ever be the same?

Carrie Roebling: 7 Steps on Finding Hope

via *NY Times*,[3] according to Carrie Roebling research

"One in 500 people in the U.S. has died from COVID. To try to trivialize it and say it's nothing, it doesn't matter, I think it's just a gross mischaracterization of what we are all living through."
—*Dr. Thomas Giordano, Baylor College of Medicine*

1. Laughter is important.

There are more than 400 cases daily in NYC, making it quite difficult to laugh. But I find places for joy. Old sitcoms. New podcasts. Anything with a laugh track will suffice. I ordered a book about the best 100 jokes and decided to read one joke aloud daily! The only jokes I remember growing up are the ones about some chicken crossing the road (to get away from the KFC kitchen), and I'm a vegetarian now, so I try to refrain from poultry discussions. I will, thank you. Don't get me wrong, I don't judge if you eat meat. I was raised a vegetarian. End of story.

---

3   nytimes.com/interactive/2021/us/new-york-covid-cases.html

2. Give yourself grace. Bad days will come.

I know about bad days. Like the day my favorite neighbor, Dana, became one of the 243 residents lost to coronavirus.[4] I know about bad days. The ones that keep you in bed, smelling dust mites and hopelessness. I know about bad days. And I let myself sit in the grief for a little while. I don't deny its existence, because it would be a cruel lie. Dana and I used to work at the paper together. I threw her baby shower. And now she's gone, and her son and husband are left behind. Those are the days that are hard to shake and clear the dusty sadness from my head. When I pick up the phone, our last picture together is saved in my favorites, and I look at it until my vision is blurred with tears. I let myself cry because crying is good. I let myself cry because tears can clear out the toxins. I let myself cry and dampen the pillowcase. Because tomorrow will come, and I must be ready to greet it.

3. Find a social support system & professional help.

Once I lost Dana, my closest friend, I needed help. I couldn't be there for her son or her husband if I didn't take care of myself first. There are over 11,000 therapists registered in New York State and 1,128[5] in Brooklyn, NY. This gave me hope because I knew the odds of finding someone to confide in would be high. To share my sad-

---

4   Approximately 6,805,271 cases have been reported. One in 243 residents have died from the coronavirus, resulting in a total of 80,109 deaths.

5   op.nysed.gov/professions/psychology/license-statistics

ness with someone outside of my small-knit (chosen) family would be essential for me to return to this family circle as a healing and whole individual. And because I spent my first years out of college as a journalist for the smallest newspapers and niche travel blogs, when my college roomie Dana told me she was having a child, I decided to lay roots near her in Brooklyn to be a part of her village. She and I found each other at Wesley when we decided to turn that homogenized and elite campus right side up! Both of us are from different cultural backgrounds, but scholarship recipients staged a weeklong protest of the classist, xenophobic, anti-Black, anti-Semitic, anti-woman, and anti-queer literature of mandatory freshman composition class.

We had three very clear demands.

1. Include two graduate trustees on the curriculum committee
2. Offer an apology from the department to the student body as a whole
3. Implement a constitution within every department to prevent this kind of racism, discrimination, and bias from being used as suitable educational resources ever again

The provost office had no idea who they were playing with. And honestly, neither did Dana and I. We just knew we were bound to each other. Allies and accomplices for each other's liberation for life. Every time I think of how we met and what we fought and overcame, I fall asleep with a small smile. I know I will wake with a brighter view. I know I will find the words to share with my therapist. I know the sun will return.

4. Meditate.

Do you know what I have in common with Lady Gaga, Oprah Winfrey, Hugh Jackman, Russell Brand, Kristen Bell, Kobe Bryant, Arianna Huffington, and John Lennon? Meditation. At first, it was just an assignment for a travel article about a retreat space centering BIPOC women in Bali. And then it was my island and solace in a lonely and chaotic world. I found meditation while visiting Bali. And I also found meditation to lighten the ten-pound brick that lodged itself between my lungs and trachea. I found meditation had the ability to help me disarm the anxiety in my chest. This is when I found meditation had the power to help me equalize the intrusive sounds. Without meditation, the noise was too silencing, and the silence was too deafening. But with meditation, deep breathing practice, and the practice of stillness, I was able to reclaim my voice. Surprising even more is that within my meditation journey, I had the compass to finally access my dreams, and my true desires, to quiet my insecurities, and finally be at peace with myself.

5. Journal instead of doomscrolling.

I look at the lines on the paper of my composition book turned journal. I stopped using my once beloved bird app a long time ago. At first, it was a place to post your thoughts and share information and vital news, and it served as the global communities' newsletter. We could share recipes for effective homemade hand sanitizer (2 parts 91–99% alcohol, 1 part aloe vera gel, and eucalyptus and peppermint oil), updated food pantry openings (everyone is eligible for food assistance regardless of income or immigration status), emergency grant applications (available for housing, artists, and students in good standing), volunteer opportunities (dog walking for the animal shelters and cat fostering openings are still in high demand), and transparent data about the true impact of the coronavirus.[6]

But that feels like a long history ago. Today, the internet has far too few funny cat memes and French bulldog videos, and far too many excessive amounts of hate speech disguised as freedom of speech. I begin to doodle in the corners as my mind paces the room. My eyes dart from line to line, and I feel a spark. My pen begins a new meditation. One that can keep me near hope and is fueled by joy.

---

6   There were more than 34.3 million known cases of COVID-19 in the United States.

6. Help others in need.

I began sewing a long time ago. First buttons on a shirt, then a tote bag and throw pillows, until finally I learned how to put my hobby of sewing to larger use. I drop off handmade face masks every week with an additional fabric swatch to house carbon filters. Sal's, the neighborhood bodega, gives them to the elders in the community. I also drop off two dozen at the women's shelter, and for the local nurse practitioner, Esme. 98.2% of those stricken by COVID-19 are known to survive.[7] I believe we can raise that number even higher, if we vow to take care of one another.

7. Listen to your body and exercise regularly.

    a. I drink water every day, even when I don't want to.

    b. I walk the neighborhood for fifteen minutes one way up and fifteen minutes one way back. I try first thing in the morning before too many people are on the streets, and I can walk freely without my face mask.

    c. I monitor my caffeine intake. I've learned to love matcha lattes as much as chamomile tea. The reduction of caffeine allows me a more restful sleep.

    d. I don't punish myself with odd diets. I eat the chocolate or the piece of fruit. Or both!

---

7   apnews.com/article/fact-checking-970830023526

Esmerelda: How Is Love Wrong?

If you have actively attempted to find your soulmate before the COVID-19 pandemic, I'm sure you can admit that it was a difficult task. But being queer and newly graduated via Zoom, and searching for a soulmate during a pandemic is three-fold impossible. My mom says, "Figure out who you are, Esmerelda, and who you like. The rest will fall into place."

For the past year, I've endured masked living, hand-sanitized living, and six-foot-distanced living, all the while searching for that special someone to share my dreams with. So not only have I been trying to figure out who I am and my purpose in the world, but I am also trying to figure out who I like. In my head is the *Jeopardy!* of dating questions, and I never seem to get it right!

Name someone who you are attracted to.
Who is my best friend, Xochitl? Who is Tariq from middle school? Who is anyone with soft eyes and an annoying laugh?

Who is the girl in the back of class whose smile makes you smile until there is a warmth in your belly, and you can't think about a day without her?

Name someone you admire.
Who is Nicole Zizi? Who is Madam CJ Walker? Who is anyone who loves to share T-shirts, and lip gloss, and stories late into the night?

These are the game-style questions that run through my head every other day, and the answers are never the same. Because every day I feel like I am not the same me. Every article I read online changes me. Every pandemic story I read online about friends and family members gone missing changes me. So I don't expect my heart not to toss, turn, and evolve constantly.

When I came out to my mom, it was nothing like I thought. And even though I worked out my speech during a pep talk with my mentor Esme the Nurse, I thought I would cry. And I thought Mom would cry. I thought Dad would come home and be upset. I didn't know what to say except "I like my friend Xochitl. I think she likes me. She makes me happy." But later that evening, when we were all eating my favorite dinner (arroz con pollo) and laughing over large glasses of sweet tea, Mom looked at me and responded, "How is love wrong?"

I remember so much warmth crawling from my chest, up my neck, past my ears, and to my cheeks.

I couldn't wait to return to school so I could finally profess my *like* to Xochitl. Unfortunately, this was the night before quarantine shushed the loudest city into a cloak of quiet. School doors closed before we ever had a chance to talk, and the FaceTime sessions between Xochitl and me became strained. But my feelings never changed; I just bottled them up inside. Xochitl moved to Long Island with her parents and two older brothers during quarantine. She couldn't be bothered with me and my "neediness," which was so odd, because we had been each other's rock. But it was undeniable that our connection was stalled when a text message thread couldn't resuscitate the easiness of our friendship. Mom said, "Esmerelda, everything changes. Trust your heart, and prepare yourself for the bounty that will arrive."

When Xochitl moved, that was that! I know I'm lucky because Xochitl ghosting me was small peanuts at a wild circus considering this was before Dad's mental health diagnosis. Before a world was turned upside down within an already upside-down world.

How is love wrong?

My father left a while ago. Not because he's an asshole or anything. But he had mental health issues that took him away from himself before any of us knew what side was at stake. Once he went missing for a week. We found him in an encampment by the Junction. Where cans and carts become a fortress for the houseless. We brought him home, got him help, and secured his medication, and for the next three years he would pop in and out of our lives. His meds made him feel too groggy, and the world never makes room for men to feel vulnerable. So he stopped taking his meds and the cycle continued: fortress break, bring him home, get him help, secure his meds, groggy, defeated, rinse in rejection, break, bring, help, secure, groggy, ghost, rinse in rejection, repeat. Until one day we couldn't find him. But we did find a note scribbled in Sharpie ink on the red lines of the yellow notebook paper. It read, "I'll be back when I can."

My mom was already a forced stay-at-home parent with SSI checks and back pains. She was holistic and prayer-forward. She tossed her OxyContin in the commode and turned to the arnica pills and natural inflammatory capsules.

After Dad's second search party, we enlisted members of our church. They all knew and loved Dad and held prayer calls for him every time he went missing. But one day during Bible study group, some of the middle school girls began picking on me for wearing my rainbow-printed shirt. "My dad got me this shirt," I said, hoping it would shut them up. But they kept on. One girl said it was a sin. Another girl said it was a sin. Another girl said it was a sin. And the Bible study leader nodded approvingly. I told Mom what happened on the way out before she made a beeline to the Bible study leader, Mr. Hence. She looked him dead in his eye and said, "How is love wrong?"

And that was it. By the time we reached Dad's third or fourth disappearance, we were our own search party of two. Mom became her own holy space. She pastored in front of the living room window every night. It was different from her prayer time. But I didn't bother her about it. I was fifteen then and couldn't care less. Since the pandemic changed the course of my life, a few things have remained consistent.

1. I graduated from high school (online),
2. I started my first job as a social media content creator (online), and
3. I experience the world through my Zoom screen (that's right, you guessed it, online).

I am stuck at home with my mom. Mom and her prayers since she's been out with worker's compensation. The vaccine is not available to the public yet, so we have to be extra careful. We only have each other, you know?

During a certificate program for my social media training, I fell in deep-like with someone. She reminded me of Xochitl, her smile sparked just the same, and we always made a point to study together. Our connection was palpable. My bedroom would swirl with glimmers of peppered laughter as we finished each other's sentences, and once, she caught me staring at her. Daydreaming during our virtual meetup began to happen so often that I think I creeped her out. She stuttered, "Wh-wh-why are you staring at me like that?" or "You're so weird! Where did you go again?"

After we graduated from the certification program, I lost touch with my crush. She stopped liking my pictures online. At first, I thought it was because she was afraid of such an overwhelming feeling of loss. There are so many examples of untimely transitions—just look at my dad. Just look out your front door. I mean, sometimes I'm afraid of being unalive too.

My mom says, "We all go, some of us just sooner than others." Gwendolyn Ewie is stirring the sugar alternative into her decaf and looking out the window when she says, "It's your job to live bright while you are here. To try and not dim your own light, or slip into a darkness that feels like death all its own. That's all you can do." She clinks her small spoon against the lip of the delicate teacup I gave her for Christmas two years ago and smiles a small smile.

My mom is the wisest woman I know. But since we've been stuck in this walk-up in Morningside Heights, she might be getting on my nerves. Just a little. I mean, she's the only person I think I really know, but sometimes I think she knows what I'm thinking before I do—and honestly, it's annoying.

Name the song that loops in your head when you are your bravest.
What is Goapele's "Closer"?

Let me paint the picture. Right after the city shut down in March, and Xochitl and I no longer kept in touch, I started talking to a girl named RiRi. We talked music on the dating app, and she was a freshman at BMCC in downtown Manhattan, so I made a point to take the train down to the white arch wings of the new World Trade Center and meet her out in the open air for the first time.

She held her iPhone speaker up near my ear and said, "You're going to love this song." While RiRi and I walked along the water on the Joe DiMaggio Highway, I knew what the familiar thrashing in my chest meant. We played Goapele, Tems, Cleo Sol, Amare Symoné, and SZA from downtown, past Little Island, the outdoor park, and finally ended at Chelsea Piers.

Her lips were soft, like bubble gum–flavored clouds. I was shocked. How much my head began to swim around the fact that our faces fit together perfectly. This was our first and last kiss.

After our hangout session, I didn't want to appear too eager. I mean, thirst is only allowed when in a desert; otherwise, one must play it cool. But after a week went by and RiRi didn't text, I texted her. The messages popped up as a green bubble, which didn't match the usual blue bubbles of our past. I thought, maybe she's traveling or in a no-service zone, or *insert flimsy excuse here.*

By week three, it was clear, RiRi went missing. Just like my dad. It pissed me off. I interrogated myself with the same line of questioning that I tortured myself with after I failed to find my father the last time.

First question (I am paranoid): Did I do something wrong?
Second question (I am angry): I mean, what the hell?
Third question (I am frantic): Come on—it's a whole pandemic.
I deserve more than being ghosted!

I heard my mom praying this morning, "Bless my daughter, my only light. Give her a good life. Keep her healthy and strong. Show her the value of her own song." Since Mom is no longer going to the Universal Unitarian for All Souls Church, she only ever paused her prayers to clang pots out the window at 7 p.m.

Her prayers and RiRi looking at my photos but not answering my texts got me vexed. So I blocked her from liking my page so I could get some work done. I mean, I do work on social media for a living.

I am hungry for someone's hand to touch. I listen to Goapele until I am sick and congested from crying. Being ghosted is one thing. But being ghosted after someone made you feel alive for the first time in your life—sucks. It has been five months of this crappy hole-in-your-heart feeling. The numbness is a certain kind of death. One that waits for you calmly in your sleep. One that waits for you on the other side of your favorite smell. I began to think Rihanna was just like the kids who made fun of me at church.

Social media doesn't help the ache.
I make a finsta account so I can see Rihanna without her know-

ing I'm watching. She's updated her page for the first time in months!

My heart skips a beat.

It's a picture of her wearing an engagement ring. I can't believe it. We're only eighteen years old! And besides, maybe I wanted to marry her? How could she not tell me she was getting engaged? The caption read, "I've waited all my life to marry my best friend. We've known each other since middle school, but we've loved each other for several lifetimes. So happy to be your wife, Jonathan."

In a panic, I write, "I hope this union brings you closer to your dreams." In a panic, I deactivate the account. *Bless my daughter, my only light. Give her a good life. Keep her healthy and strong. Show her the value of her own song.* I close my phone and answer the five pings from my email account. All social media assets that need captioning and to be published by 5 p.m. Pacific. It's already 3 p.m. Eastern, so that means I only have five hours to get the task completed. After scouring the internet for phrases that aren't overly used, I hit send on the assignment—forty minutes before deadline. Invigorated, I forget I haven't been kissed in five months. I haven't held a hand besides my own mother's during our dinner table food blessings. And honestly, it's getting old. *Bless my daughter, my only light. Give her a good life. Keep her healthy and strong. Show her the value of her own song.*

Today I am eighteen. I choose to celebrate my birthday by ordering a pair of brand-new platinum sneakers. I don't unbox until today. I want something to look forward to while my mom cooks my favorite meal.

The shoes sit in a red-and-white box. When I flip the lid back, all I can think is "What an astronaut's dream." Honestly, I would never have the courage to wear them before now—but something about the finality of Rihanna's engagement ring. She called him her best friend? I thought we were best friends? I thought she loved me or at least respected me enough to give a warning about her *other* best friend and their blossoming love. I would never have the courage to buy these blingy orbs.

I strut up and down the hallway just to feel something other than numbness. In a panic, I opened my phone and re-downloaded an app I had abandoned when I thought Rihanna and I were in deep love. I sign up for a new account on Slant, a dating app for pandemic queer love connections. After making my account as brief and to the point as possible, I add a selfie and post it under the handle @UptownLucent. I try not to think of Rihanna's ring. I try not to dive into the pool that is sadness, even though it is a perfect temperature for sulking. Instead, I scroll through the Slant app while my mom's prayers calm me. *Bless my daughter.* I scroll, swipe, swipe, scroll, star, star, and swipe before I close the app. *My only light. Give her a good life.*

I walk into the kitchen for the first serving of my birthday wish. Mom smiles and slowly walks back to her perch in front of the living room window. *Keep her healthy and strong. Show her the value of her own song.*

It is weeks later. And I've been fasting from my phone. I drink green tea with Mom, I freelance virtually, and wear my silver linings like jewelry to the bodega for a re-up on oatmeal, oat milk, and brown sugar. At the checkout line, I have time to open my phone and scroll through the app. It's the first time I've opened it since the panic. There are two messages. The app is wild. If you friend the person, you can tell the distance of your Slant Crush by the red dot, orange dot, and yellow dot next to their name. A red dot means they are offline. The orange dot means they are available to chat. And the yellow dot means they are in your four-block vicinity. It doesn't allow you to become a stalker or anything—but it does pique your interest and make it more likely that you will try to meet this connection in real life. If even you know you are near someone—to know you can look at the same part of the sky together—is warming.

I click open the message and after reading a haiku about my selfie looking like a sunset's rival, I heart their profile. *Cheesy,* I reply before adding, *and beautiful. Thank you.* I float out the doors with my purchases and up the stairs. The day shimmers by. Months later, I didn't open the app, not once. I've been far too busy with Mom and the anti-search for my dad. The app shows me that Cheesy Poet has sent several messages.

September 2020 Cheesy: I'm sorry I ghosted you. I was afraid of telling my parents and I didn't want to disappoint them. I also didn't want to disappoint you. I'm sorry. Call me when you get this. Maybe we can talk fr fr?

October 2020 Cheesy: I guess I deserve this. But I just want my friend back. You were the only one I could talk to. I took you for granted. I'm sorry. I hope you can forgive me. Have you listened to our song lately? I listen to it every single day. It's almost like you are with me. I wish I could kiss you again.

November 2020 Cheesy: I can't tell if you've been online or not. But I can see that you haven't read these messages. I tried to call your old number with no luck. I won't give up. Not until you tell me to. I'm back in town if you ever want to go watch the airplanes take off? I miss you.

Three months of me not checking this app and I realized Cheesy Poet is actually Rihanna. The space in my chest feels so bright, you would've thought the ozone layer peeled a part of itself open and boiled my icy heart. At first all I can think about is the warm goodness when someone you like a lot finally gives you the attention you've been dreaming of! But then I think, I need to be with someone who really wants me for the long haul, and not when times are good and easy.

I close the app. I have to figure out what I want to say. I want to be friends with Rihanna again, but not like this. For the first time in a long time, I put my needs first. There is nothing wrong with boundaries. And my boundaries were simple: no ghosting.

The world is so full of vanishing, and I couldn't afford for someone to leave me holding a carbonated bottle of feelings, shaken and placed back into my hands ready to explode. I turn off my phone and call towards the kitchen, where I hear my mom making a cup of decaf.

"Hey, Mom, I found a link for your church online. Would you like to watch the service together?"

She clanks her spoon in the sink and beams over her shoulder, surprised. "That would be wonderful, dear. I need to be prayed for too, you know?" She rinses the sink and replaces the fallen silver into the dish rack. And I know exactly what she means.

We all need someone to treat us like we are worth picking up polished.

So I delete the app off my phone and head to the laptop to screen-share on the living room TV screen. I know what I deserve. I just want someone who won't turn away from my love. I want someone who always makes me feel like I'm shining.

Chorus: Electra on Love

Eff di pandemic teach wi anyting, it is that you never know what it's like to waak a mile eena smaddy else shoes. Suh nuh taak bout di pebble roads dem live on. It easy to call people names. Dem play reindeer games before we learn de sickness don't pick favorites.
Even de rich people dem fraid a sickness, cause dem can't buy immunity fi demself!

Eff di pandemic teach wi anyting, it is you never remember the things you didn't get to do when you are grieving the person you never get to become. Coughs cleaned di air like an old mop in a airport bathroom stall. What is clean air?

Eff di pandemic teach wi anyting, it is this: Love is for every single soul. Di squirrel with the bagel in Prospect Park. Di houseless family pitching a tent in Tompkins Square. Di auntie who wait for her meals to be delivered. Di young ballplayer with a blue face mask on

his upper forearm, dribbling down the court like a promise towards
tomorrow.

Tell me the truth, Electra. What does love have to do with
COVID-19?

Everyting.
Love open our eyes each morning, our eyes touch the sky, the sky touch
the sun, the sun touch the trees, the trees touch the air, and the air fill
up our lungs. That sound like love to me.
I mean, love is not a vaccine. But when we take care of one another,
man . . . Love is the cure.

Maseo Craig Sr.: Hope Is an Act of Liberation

We are here today, friends, on this ledge of tomorrow, with one question: "How do we assure there is no one left behind?" When I say "no one," I am speaking about the city workers. When I say "no one," I am speaking about health care workers. When I say "no one," I am speaking about the underpaid and overworked. Your nannies who work for less than they deserve. Your office delivery people who work for unlivable minimum wages.

We are here today because we are not interested in being rich! We are here today because we are interested in justice!

Justice for all creates safe housing. Justice provides equal education for all. But when we work as a cog in the wheel of capitalism, we are laughing in the face of justice. We are looking at Justice's imbalanced scale and shrugging. Because solidarity isn't solidarity when one of us is without; affordable and clean housing should be our right as citizens. Free and low-cost health care should be our right. Safety in all our communities should be our right. We should be creating generational wealth among our communities, not just those born into money. We should be curing systemic oppressions and watch all waters rise.

When you win, I win! When you eat, I eat. When you dream, we all find a way for rich colors and sounds to exist! When you dream, we all have a blueprint for flying!

Police brutality and mass incarceration should be a mirage. A long-ago nightmare! Not a means to make money off the pain, addiction, and impoverishment of a people.

I know, I know, you believe that is a tall order. Sounds more like too many politics and not enough people! I agree! Now, listen here, I am not in the business of politics. But I am in the business of helping people. I am in the business of watching all of our children prosper and grow. All of our children!

Black, Hispanic and Latin Americans, Alaska
Natives, Chinese, Arab, Asian Americans, Indians
and Native Americans, Africans, Pakistanis,
Vietnamese, Filipinos, Cubans, and Whites. All of
our children deserve a brighter horizon than the one
we promised at the end of some mythical golden
road! This country can hold us all firmly! This
country can hold us all!

Now, if you ask my wife, Symone, she will say there
are food deserts that should be flooded with fresh
vegetables and fruit. She will say that after-school
child care should be readily available for all. She
would say breakfast and healthy school lunches
should be free of charge to any of our children in
need. She would argue for useful and new books for
each student in every class, and would also say I am
talking your ears off.

She is the most brilliant woman I know. So I will
be brief and leave you with this. We can hope the
wealthy hear our cries. Or we can make them listen!
If you drive a bus, stop. If you operate a train, stop.
If you provide for the wealthy and you are owed for
your labor but have only promises to show for it in
the form of past-due notices, stop. We will not wait
for them to give us what is rightfully ours—we will
take it! If the rich feed on the work of the poor, then

how will the poor eat? I say, burn it all down—begin again!

One nation, one table.

Let no one leave the kitchen hungry!

Chorus: Hyacinth's Farewell

I hope you have the common sense to stand up for what's right. That's the last thing I said to Yusef. And I meant it. 'Cause it was the last thing my nana said to me.

Yusef hasn't always made the best decisions, but he's a good kid. "I hope you have the common sense" was my way of saying "You are so smart, Yusef! Don't let them make you believe you are less than." I mean, we all make mistakes, right? Some of our mistakes catch up to us before we even caught our breath.

I mean. When the pandemic shows the mistake of how they rolled out vaccines, and how they didn't keep all communities safe—when the history book turns a mirror back to this moment, the adults have a lot of explaining to do.

The pandemic arrived and reminded us we all have one thing in common: We Must Live.

Listen to young people, we know more than you can realize. We have ideas about what is next. And we've been taking notes from adults for years! Which is to say, you can learn a thing or two from us!

Before we lost my nana to her painful breathing of COVID-19, she asked me to write her a poem. She said, "Give me something to think about while I rest my eyes."

And I'm a little shy, because I'm not as good as Symphony, but I would never leave my nana waiting. So I tried my best. I go . . .

Hyacinth: We, a Litany on Surviving

After Audre Lorde

We young & we still wise
We learned from our parents' mistakes and grow
We create and become the freedom our elders fought to
    achieve
We dream in color and we believe in science

We climate justice
We trans rights
We women's rights
We immigration rights
We anti-war
We poverty abolitionist
We love without borders and beyond binaries
We able-bodied and disabled
We mental health day and debrief
We pass the plate and lift while we climb
We laugh without cutting one another down

We not the mean and bully brigade, you can sit at our
    table
We laugh until our jokes create gardens of dreams
We dance to the staccato of soca and house
We bubble gum before bedtime and lullabies
We migrant stories and homemade recipes
We thrift culture
We meditate
We respect our elders with open dialogue
We respect ourselves with tough questions and grace
We graceful and grateful
We clumsy humans with piercings
We vaccinated with cartoons on repeat
We chicken noodle soup with a bevvy on the side
We activate our goodwill and share our hand sanitizer
We mask up and keep calm
We are a generous legacy
Just trying to make our ancestors proud
            even when our backs are against the wall.

A List of Acknowledgments

1. I wrote this as a recollection of one of our lives' hardest times.

2. I thank the fellowships and residencies that made the editing and synthesizing processes possible. Much love to the spaces ALL ARTS, Baldwin for the Arts, Casa Ecco, Lincoln Center, National Black Theatre, and Ucross.

3. Thank you, NYC. Each borough is a vein that returns blood to our hearts. You brim with stories; I am so lucky to bear witness.

4. Thank you, young people, for inspiring these conversations and for demanding I remain brave.

5. Thank you for buying this book. Thank you, friends, comrades, mentors, and students turned teachers, for putting eyes on it.

6. The squad who keeps me afloat, I love you. I continue because of your care. Big love to Jive Poetic and Amari, Adam Falkner, Deesha Philyaw, Sarah Kay, Jon Sands, Noah Arhm Choi, Jason Reynolds, Jordana Leigh, Ayana Walker, Sofia Snow, Charlotte Sheedy and Sheedy Lit Agency, Jacqueline Woodson, Caroline Rothstein, Jarmal Harris, and Ana Paula and Anya of Blue Flower Arts. And to Shelly Ann Panton, for vetting the Jamaican patois. Forever grateful for my editor, Phoebe Yeh. Thank you for fighting for me and these stories.

If it were 7 p.m., I would clang my pots for the essential workers and my ancestors who made this collection possible.

About the Author

Mahogany L. Browne, a Kennedy Center Next 50 fellow, is a writer, playwright, organizer, and educator. Browne received fellowships from ALL ARTS, Arts for Justice, AIR Serenbe, Baldwin for the Arts, Cave Canem, Hawthornden, Poets House, Mellon Research, Rauschenberg, Wesleyan University, and Ucross. Browne's books include *Vinyl Moon, Chlorine Sky* (optioned for Steppenwolf Theatre), *Black Girl Magic,* and banned books *Woke: A Young Poet's Call to Justice* and *Woke Baby.* Browne's Chrome Valley tour was highlighted in *Publishers Weekly* and the *New York Times.* Founder of the diverse lit initiative Woke Baby Book Fair, Browne is the 2024 Paterson Poetry Prize winner. She holds an honorary doctor of philosophy degree awarded by Marymount Manhattan College, and is the inaugural poet in residence at the Lincoln Center. Mahogany lives in Brooklyn, New York.

mobrowne.com